BURIED

WHITE HAVEN WITCHES (BOOK 1)

MAGIC

TJ GREEN

Buried Magic

Mountolive Publishing

Copyright © 2018 TJ Green

ISBN 978-0-9951163-0-6

Cover Design by Fiona Jayde Media

Editing by Missed Period Editing

To My Mother - Thank You

Contents

Prologue

We are witches, born from generations of witches, and our magic has been passed down through the centuries.

But it seems we have more power than we ever thought possible.

When things that were hidden come to light, an enemy is awakened. Our ancient grimoires were hidden for a reason; now we are in a race to find them first.

One

A very always liked to read the tarot cards on a full moon, outside if the weather allowed, and today it did. It was mid-June and hot. The earth smelled rich, and the scent of lavender drifted towards her.

She sat at her garden table. The brick-paved patio area was flooded with silvery light and the garden beyond was full of plants, lost in the shadows despite the full moon. The only things visible were the white roses that nodded from the depths of the borders, and the gravel paths that snaked around them.

Earlier that day she had sensed a shift in the normal path of her life; a premonition that required further investigation. Out of long practice she sat calmly, shuffling the cards and then placing them out in the cross before her, turning them one by one. She shuddered. Change was coming, and with it, danger. The cards revealed it and she could feel it. And it would happen soon.

Avery leaned back, perplexed, and then jumped slightly as she heard the click of the gate. Alex, another witch. She recognised his scent and sound. Her worry over the reading was replaced by curiosity.

He stepped into view, his expression invisible with the moon behind him, casting her in shadow. He was tall, with broad shoulders and a lean, muscular build. It was like a wall had stepped between her and the moon.

"What do you want, Alex?"

"What a lovely greeting, Avery," he said, his voice smooth. He pulled a chair out and sat opposite her, looking down at the cards. "So you sense it, too."

"Sense what?"

"You know what." He sounded impatient. "That something is coming. Don't you think we should work together?"

"No."

He leaned back, shifting slightly so that the moon lit his face, showing his day-old stubble and his long dark hair that fell just below his shoulders. His brown eyes looked black in the light. "This is ridiculous. You have no reason to distrust me."

She refused to be drawn. "I have no reason to trust you, either. You disappeared for years, and now you're back. I have no idea who you even are anymore."

"I'm the same witch I always was. People travel, you know. That's life!"

Even now Alex could make her blood boil with his infuriating superiority. She wanted to throw something at him, like a lightning bolt. "Why are you here?"

They stared at each other across the table, Avery only able to see a glint of moonlight in his eyes, until he said with forced patience, "There are five witches now in White Haven, five of us who wield the old magic. We should meet. Pool our resources. I can't believe you haven't already."

"We've had no need to form a coven, and I like working alone." She inwardly chastised herself. Why did she have to sound so defensive? It was okay to work alone.

"I've been talking to Elspeth. She'd like to form one."

Avery rolled her eyes. "Of course she would."

"There's nothing wrong with that! We can share ideas, share our strengths."

"We're all witches! What do we need to share?"

"Oh, let me see," he said with a sigh. "El can work metal, brilliantly, metal and gems, in fact. Far better than any of us can. Have you seen what she's been producing lately?"

"No."

"You should. And of particular use for us, she can weave magic into an Athame, and other useful objects we use in our rituals."

"I can do that, too," she said impatiently, "we all can. We're witches."

"Not as good as she can," he persisted. "And Briar is excellent at using herbs and healing. Better than all of us," he said, cutting her off before she could protest. "Gil is particularly good at using water magic. And then there's you." He stopped and just looked at her, his expression unfathomable. He was making her uncomfortable.

"What about me?" She was annoyed with him for being so very logical, and she felt the wind stirring around her as her annoyance increased.

He laughed, the white of his teeth bright against his shadowed face. He looked around and the breeze made strands of his hair float around his face. "Am I making you cross? I'm sure you're causing that wind."

She frowned and cut it off, the wind dying instantly.

"Air. You manipulate it so easily. And new spells, your intuitiveness—those are your strengths."

She was so unnerved at his knowledge of her that she responded with sarcasm. "And what about you, Alex? What can *you* bring?"

"My ability to scry, to prophecise, my astral abilities. And fire." He glanced at the candle that sat on the side of the table, unlit, and it suddenly flared to life, the flame shooting a foot into the air before it settled down to a small, orange flame. The light illuminated his grin. "I burn hot, Avery. Nice on cold nights."

"How lovely," she said, trying to dispel the images that rushed into her head. She put the flame out as quickly as he had lit it, the smoke eddying between them.

He leaned forward. "I'm calling a meeting. The others should know that we've sensed something. We need to be on our guard. My place, tonight at ten." He stood, once again blocking the moon briefly before he headed to the gate, his gait long. "By the way, your defences on the house need strengthening. See you later, Avery."

Alex was 29, a year older than her, and they'd been to the same schools and shared the same powers, and yet he infuriated her. She watched him go, then looked up at the moon and wanted to scream, but the moon counselled silence, so she swept the cards up, shuffled, and dealt again.

Two

Avery woke at dawn after a restless sleep, the barely-there light filtering through the blinds in the bedroom. She had been thinking more about Alex than the ominous reading, and that annoyed her more than anything. She hated the way he just slid into her mind and stayed there.

By the time she got to work she felt irritable. Work was a bookshop called Happenstance Books, which she'd inherited from her grandmother, along with the building it was in. They stocked new and old books, fiction, non-fiction, and the esoteric—witchcraft, divination, angels, devils, and all things in between, as well as tarot cards, incense, greeting cards, postcards, and other occult-related objects. The shop was well placed, halfway up a small side street that wound up from the sea, and wedged between a coffee shop and a gift store selling local trinkets to tourists. It was stacked with high shelves that wound around the walls, as well as through the middle, making the interior a section of narrow passages. A selection of comfy chairs and a small sofa were placed in strategic locations to encourage reading and lingering, and it smelt pleasantly of old paper, coffee, and incense.

Sally, her friend and the store manager, was already in their stock room at the rear of the shop, unpacking a box of old books Avery had brought a week ago in a house sale. She knew Avery was a witch, although she never called her one. It was inevitable she should know after their years of friendship, although Avery made out it was something far more wishy-washy than it really was and Sally indulged her accordingly.

Sally looked up and smiled. "You're early! Someone kick you out of bed?"

"Funny! Bad night's sleep. What about you?"

"You know me, always an early bird. Coffee's on if you want some."

"I don't want some, I *need* some!" she said, heading to the small galley kitchen, inhaling the coffee fumes gratefully. She hesitated a moment and then called out, "Alex came to see me last night."

There was a moment of silence as the rustling of books stopped, and Sally came to the door, leaning against the frame. "I thought you didn't get on?"

"We don't, sort of. But he sensed the same thing as me." She looked at her, trying to decide what to say. In the end she just said it all. "I was reading the cards last night and I thought I saw something. Something dark. I have no idea what, but Alex saw it, too. He came to talk. At two in the morning!"

"So he knew you'd be up," Sally said, raising her eyebrows quizzically. "Have you two got some psychic link?"

Avery shook her head, leaned back against the counter, and sipped her coffee. Sweet and strong, just as she liked it. She might just start to feel human soon. "No! At least I hope not. It's very disconcerting."

Sally shuffled against the doorframe. "I like him, I don't really get why you don't. He's honest, and runs a great pub! He's got a fab chef at the moment. Have you been?"

"No, not since he arrived."

"Are you sure nothing's happened between you two?"

Avery rolled her eyes. "No. Anyway, he wants to talk at his pub tonight. He's calling a meeting with the others." Sally would know exactly whom she meant by the others.

"It's probably a good idea," Sally nodded. "There's strength in numbers."

"Oh, don't you start."

Sally grinned, raking her hand through her blonde hair. "I wouldn't hesitate if Alex invited me over. He's very good-looking."

"And he knows it. And besides, you're married with two kids!"

Sally married her childhood sweetheart when she was 20 years old, and within a couple of years they had their first child, swiftly followed by a second. Avery had no idea how she managed the shop and her home life so efficiently.

"I meant, if I was single!" Sally changed tack, looking slightly worried. "So, is this serious, what you and Alex saw? You've never mentioned anything like this before."

Avery immediately regretted saying anything, and shook her head. "No, probably not. I've probably got a rival with a new bookstore opening. I'm sure it will be fine. It was just sort of spooky, Alex turning up when he did, and I've probably read more into it than I should have. Anyway, anything good in that box?"

Sally headed back to the store room, Avery trailing after her, and pulled a book out of the box she'd been unpacking. "Old editions of the classics, but nothing riveting. Not yet, anyway. I've got to do another house visit later. Unless you want to? One of us has to update our inventory." She had a smirk on her face, knowing Avery hated doing the inventory.

Avery smiled sweetly, "I'd love to pick up those boxes! Thanks Sally. Where am I going?"

"Do you remember that little old lady who used to come in here sometimes? Anne? She was a bit of a local historian."

"Yeah, I think so." Avery kept it light, but she did remember her. People poking about in the town's history always made her worried. She didn't want them to turn up anything she'd rather keep hidden. She'd been polite to Anne, but had otherwise tried to keep her distance.

"Well, she died the other week, and she's left us some books."

"Oh," Avery suddenly felt bad and also slightly relieved. "I'm sorry to hear that. Sure, I'll go. Who arranged it?"

"Her son, Paul. I haven't met him, he just phoned. I arranged to pick up mid-morning, at her house. Are you all right, Avery? You look a bit odd."

The feeling of unease had rushed back like an incoming tide and Avery felt dizzy. "No, I'm fine, bad night's sleep, remember? Need more coffee." She headed back to the kitchen, trying to subdue her worry.

Avery pulled up outside a large, old house that sat on a rise overlooking the sea on the edge of the town. The second she saw it she felt a shudder pass through her. Something had alerted her witchy senses, something magical. It was only a trace, but it was there.

She looked at the house thoughtfully. Anne hadn't presented any inkling of magic, so why could she sense something here? And what of her son, Paul? They certainly weren't related to the other four witches in the town, and she was pretty sure there weren't any others. Was this a trap? But surely if he'd been a witch he'd have tried to disguise the wisps of magic she could sense.

The house was built from the mellow, creamy stone that many houses in the area were built from, and that also made up the old boundaries snaking across fields and along roadsides. It sat down a drive that was overgrown with bushes and trees. The paving was cracked, the paint on the door and window frames was peeling off, and the whole place looked like it needed a complete overhaul. At one point, this house would have been one of the most coveted houses in White Haven, and probably would be again after a ton of money had been thrown at it. She looked down the lane. All of the other houses here were in much better condition. She bet the neighbours were looking forward to the renovation. But was something hiding behind that cracked facade?

She sat for a few minutes, watching the house and trying to detect if there was a threat, but other than the whiff of magic, she sensed nothing.

Avery looked in the rear view mirror and checked her appearance. Her long, red hair was loose and relatively neat, and her pale green eyes had lost the tiredness from earlier in the day. *Coffee was awesome.* She touched up her makeup, grabbed her phone and checked there weren't any messages, then exited her old green Bedford van, something else she'd inherited from her gran, locking it behind her. She smoothed her long, dark blue maxi dress, keen to make a good impression.

As she walked up the drive, she scanned around the garden, but noted nothing unusual until she came to the front door where a vigorous pot of thyme and one of sage was placed either side of the door. Common plants, but they also offered protection. And on the corner of the doorframe she saw a small mark. Another symbol of protection.

This was getting weirder. She rang the doorbell and waited for a few seconds, flexing her fingers in case she needed to defend herself, before finally hearing footsteps approaching. The door swung open to reveal a harried-looking man who appeared to be in his sixties. He looked at her, confused.

"Can I help you?"

"I'm Avery, from Happenstance Books. You must be Paul? You asked me to collect your mother's books—Anne Somersby? Is this a good time?" She smiled encouragingly.

"Oh, yes, sorry, of course. I'm a little distracted—I'm sorting through some paperwork. Come in, please." He leaned forward and shook her hand. "Just follow me and I'll show you the library." He laughed, "Well, it's not really a library, but it does have a lot of books."

Avery relaxed slightly. She didn't detect anything magical or threatening from him. He walked ahead of her, leading her down the long hallway to a room at the back of the house, looking out onto extensive gardens.

She paused at the window, "Wow, what a beautiful garden."

He laughed, "It *was* a beautiful garden. Now it's a mess."

She laughed, too. "Well, you know what I mean. It will be again." She looked around the room she was in, "And this is amazing, too!"

"You're a book lover. I just see more stuff I have to move. But yes. It is."

The ceilings were high, and the room was lined with heavy oak shelves filled with books. The small amount of exposed bare wall was panelled with the same dark oak. And the magical something was here—Avery could sense it more strongly now. She tried to contain her excitement, schooling her face carefully. "Did Anne leave me all of these?"

He gestured around the room, "Everything, although of course, you don't have to take them all." He looked puzzled. "Did you know her well?"

Avery shuffled awkwardly. "If I'm honest, not really. She came into the shop, chatted sometimes, bought books." She shrugged. "I'm guessing that's why she left them to me—to bring them back home. I'm sorry to hear she died."

Paul smiled sadly. "Thank you, but she'd had a rich life." He gestured at the shelves. "There were some old town histories she'd put together herself that she particularly wanted you to have. Insisted, in fact, before she died. Made me promise I wouldn't forget. Are you a history fan, too?"

Avery tried to cover her surprise with a small lie. "Very much so. You can't live in White Haven without loving history. We sell a lot of history books in my shop."

Paul laughed, "Quite a murky history, in places! What with witches, caves, smuggling, and wrecks at sea—the place is riddled with strange deeds!"

Avery's heart had skipped at beat at the mention of witches, and she laughed along with him, feeling the hair rise on the back of her neck. "True, but no more so than many old villages along the coast, I guess."

Paul nodded. "Anyway, I better get on. I'll be in the study going through more papers." He sighed. "She accumulated everything, you know. Would you like coffee?"

"Yes please, sounds great. Black, two sugars."

He disappeared, and for a second Avery stood still, thinking, while her heart pounded uncomfortably. She sensed magic, and Anne had requested she come here. *Had she known what she was?* She couldn't think about that now. She turned back to the books. It took all her self-control not to run over and start pulling them from the shelves.

Something was definitely here; her witchy senses were tingling all over. She quickly scanned the shelves. They were crammed with old, worn paperbacks, hardbacks, and books with old leather covers—a mixture of classics, romances, thrillers, and reference books. She focused on where she could feel the pull of magic, and looked up.

There, in the far corner, on a top shelf, was a row of old leather-bound books. Just as she was about to pull a chair out to use as a step, the door opened and Paul came in with her coffee.

"See anything you like?" he asked, as he put the coffee on a side table.

"Lots of thrillers and classics that would sell well, and some of the reference books, too." She tried to keep the excitement out of her voice. "Where else did your mother get her books from, do you know?"

"No idea! And I imagine she got them years ago. She didn't go out much as she got older." He looked at the dust and general dilapidation of the room with its dated decoration. "I don't think she did much of anything, except look at family trees. You probably know that she was a bit of a local historian. She would go to the library and look at the archives, and then she got a computer and would do what she could on there." He brightened at the thought and smiled. "I was quite impressed when she got a computer. She didn't let age stop her learning!" He pointed at the shelves. "The files she particularly wanted you to have are in that section. She was especially interested in old families of the area. You'll probably find them amongst that lot."

Researching old families? That gave her another prick of unease. Her family, Alex's, and Gil's would have been amongst the oldest. All magical. All with secrets. "I'll look out for them."

"Sorry, you'll have to contend with a lot of dust."

"It's fine. I'm used to it. I clear quite a few books from old houses."

He nodded, "Okay, I'll leave you to it."

As soon as he'd gone, she pulled the chair out and stood on it, reaching up to the row of books. As she pulled a few volumes out, dust billowed around her and she coughed and blinked. Grabbing a handful of them, she carried them to the table under the window. The names gave nothing away: *A Reference Book of Wildflowers, The Cave Systems of the West Country, Herbs and their Properties, English Folklore, Legends of the South.* Not what she was expecting, but interesting. She picked up a few and flicked through them. Nothing interesting. Then she picked up the book on cave systems and shook it, and a black and white photo fell to the floor, releasing the scent of magic.

She picked it up and held it under the light, and almost dropped it with shock. The photo was of a house, slightly unfocused, the gardens manicured, and a big bank of trees behind it. In front of the house were a woman and two small children staring at the camera, unsmiling and grim. But it was unmistakable. She knew that house—it belonged to Gil. *Was that his mother? No,* she corrected herself. The photo was too old. It must be his grandmother, maybe even great-grandmother? And the children must be either his mother or father, and an aunt or uncle. She could never remember whom he inherited his magic from.

After the shock, her initial reaction was one of disappointment. Gil was a witch—maybe the photo had come from his house? Was that why she could sense magic? She turned the photo over to reveal a scrawl of writing that looked like it had been written in a hurry. *"The real Jacksons."*

Her hands shook and she looked around the room as if she was being spied on. She had known Gil all her life. She liked him, a lot. He seemed so trustworthy, and now she had doubts running through her mind. This suggested that Gil was not a real Jackson. And if that was the case, who was he?

Three

A very lived in White Haven, a small seaside town on the Cornish coast. It was an old and charming place, with its old stone buildings with mullioned windows, tiny lanes, cobbled streets, quayside views, and boutique shops and restaurants, all swirling down to the sea, where fishing boats bobbed in the harbour. Outside the shops and pubs were hanging baskets and potted plants, and the whole place was picturesque. Beyond the town were rolling downs heading up and away from the sea.

This was the place she called home, a place that was filled with magic. It had a special quality to it, like a few of the ancient towns and villages that carried their old magic through the years. Many sensed it, and it attracted new agers, wiccans, mediums, pagans, and spiritualists, although she doubted that any knew that real witches actually lived among them.

It was now nearly 10:00pm, her tea of beans on toast was hours ago, and she was starving again. Part of her wished she'd gone to the pub with Sally for their usual post-work drinks with friends, but she had really wanted to read Anne's notes before meeting the other witches.

The traffic was always nightmarish in town, so she walked from her shop down to the pub, thinking about Alex and trying to dispel the annoying feelings he always provoked.

She'd always felt he thought he was better than her, and she'd re-
sented him for it. A few years ago he'd left White Haven, and she had
no idea why or where he'd been. He'd returned a few months ago,
taking over the old pub on the quayside that belonged to his uncle,
and it had been a shock to see him back. She'd seen little of him since
his return, other than when he came into her shop to say he was back.
It surprised her that he thought to tell her. He was as good-looking as
always, more so now that he was older. He'd looked around her shop,
waiting for her to be free, and then he sauntered over to the counter,
grinning. "Long time, no see, Avery. Thought I'd let you know I'm
back, in case you ever need anything."

"Thanks, Alex. Very generous of you. But I think I'll be okay."

"Same old Avery. When you change your mind, you know where to
find me." And then he strolled out the door.

Since then she'd bumped into him at a few parties, and in a few bars
with mutual friends where they'd chatted a few times, but that was
all. And yet last night he'd come to see her, had known she would have
seen something coming.

The Wayward Son, Alex's pub, was on one of the quayside roads,
looking over the small harbour with its collection of fishing boats. She
could smell the brine. It always made her tingle.

As she walked in, the sound of chatter and music swelled around
her; the pub was packed. She headed to the bar and saw Alex make his
way towards her from the far end, leaving his two bartenders to attend
to the other customers. His dark hair was tied back, but he still hadn't
shaved; dark stubble coated his chin and cheeks. He wore a black t-shirt
and old jeans, and he looked way too good. "Evening," he said, a lazy
grin on his face. "What's your poison?"

"A very large glass of red, please. And a packet of cheese and onion
crisps."

He reached behind him and grabbed a bottle of merlot. "I predict the lady likes a full red with a hint of spice. Sound good?"

"Perfect, thank you," she said, feeling churlishness wouldn't be a good idea in his pub.

"Drink's on the house, and don't worry about the crisps, there's food upstairs."

"Is there?" she asked, all animosity towards him temporarily forgotten.

"Of course, I like to feed my guests." He gestured towards the stairs at the back of the pub. "Head up, I'll be with you soon. You'll have to unlock the door, but you know how," and he promptly turned to another customer.

She grabbed her glass and headed through the crowded main room to the back, as instructed. A set of stairs was tucked to the rear of the small room that looked out onto the beer garden. Outside a breeze bustled around the courtyard garden, jostling the strings of fairy lights that lit up the drinkers still sitting outside. The back room was much quieter and darker than the main part of the pub, lit only by more fairy lights, candles on tables, and discreet up-lighting in the corners. It seemed that only locals were in here, and she nodded in greeting to a few she recognised.

She headed up the stairs and onto a broad landing, shrouded in shadows, and found a locked door. She whispered a spell to unlock it, and hearing the lock click, she turned the handle and went in.

Avery knew Alex had the whole of the first floor to himself. He didn't rent any of the rooms out, saying it was too much work, but she had never seen it before and she was surprised at how good it looked. He had knocked through as many walls as safety allowed, and consequently his flat was large and roomy, with an open plan kitchen and living area, exposed brick walls, and a massive fireplace. A tan leather sofa, enormous and squashy, dominated the living area, and a large rug covered the polished floorboards. She was impressed. Alex had style. Taking advantage of being the first there, she had a quick peek around and found there was a single bedroom leading off and a bathroom, and that was it.

Drawn by the thought of food, she headed to the kitchen, and found a few covered dishes of crackers, olives, and pickles. She nibbled a few olives and sipped her wine, wondering where the others were, but within seconds the door opened and Briar arrived, halting with surprise when she saw Avery in the kitchen.

Briar was about the same age as Avery, late-twenties, with hazel eyes and chestnut brown hair that fell in waves past her shoulders. She was petite, barely past five feet, and slim. She wore lace and lots of white and pastel shades, and of all of the witches was not only the best with herbs and potions, but also at healing. Briar sold creams and lotions, herbal medicines, and old remedies in her shop, Charming Balms Apothecary. She had deliberately made it old-fashioned and everyone loved it, especially because her stuff worked. Skin did look better, eyes were brighter, nails were stronger, old ailments were eased. The magic was subtle, but it was there.

There was something very soft and gentle about Briar, usually. Avery detected a slight prickle to her at the moment, however. She shut the door behind her and said, "So you came! I really didn't expect you would."

Avery felt a bit shocked. *Was she that unsociable?* She gave a half-smile. "I wasn't sure I would either, but here I am." She wondered if Briar was put out. "How are you? It's been a while."

"I'm fine, Avery. Just busy. The shop is very popular at the moment. Can't complain, it's summer season. It will slow down soon enough."

"I know what you mean," Avery nodded. "I've been busy, too."

Briar didn't waste time. She leaned against the counter from the living room side, sipping her white wine. "So what's this meeting about? It must be important, you don't normally come here."

The word 'normally' gave Avery a jolt. "No, I don't," she answered. "But Alex insisted."

Briar laughed. "And when has that ever made a difference?"

Before she could answer, Gil, Elspeth, and Alex arrived together, bringing in a jumble of laughter and chatter.

Alex looked surprised. "Great, you're here too, Briar! I didn't see you arrive."

"You were busy," she said, hugging him. "Simon served me."

Avery was already feeling like the outsider; they all looked pretty comfortable together. She wondered if it showed when Elspeth came round the counter into the kitchen and hugged her.

It had been a while since Avery had seen her, and she'd forgotten how gorgeous she was. Elspeth was tall and graceful, with long blonde, almost white hair that cascaded down her back. She always wore red lipstick that looked even brighter against her pale skin, but she also wore lots of jewellery. Rings, a nose piercing, necklaces, and lots of bangles, and she nearly always wore skinny black jeans, biker boots, and rock t-shirts. Elspeth owned a jewellery shop, and sold her own designs as well as things she brought in. All of her jewellery had a little magic woven through it. She sold charms and amulets that really worked, as well as pendants, rings, earrings, hair clips, pins, and brooches. She had spelled positive energies into them, and used gemstones as well. She must be making more things lately, from what Alex had said.

"Avery! It's great you're here. Alex said you were coming, but I didn't believe him."

"Elspeth, hi," she managed to murmur through the hug.

"El, please, not Elspeth! I love your hair, Avery, it's such a beautiful colour."

"Thank you," she said, suddenly conscious of her long, dark red hair.

In contrast, Gil stood next to El looking quite homely. He was shorter than Alex, his short dark brown hair was neat, and he wore a plain t-shirt and dark blue jeans. Gil ran a plant nursery called Greenlane Nursery out of the extensive grounds of his house, and it was very popular. He employed half a dozen locals, supplying hanging baskets to shops and businesses, and helped White Haven to compete in an annual garden competition, Britain in Bloom. He sold the usual annuals, perennials, and shrubs, but he specialised in herbs. Gil's family were rich and he had inherited the house and grounds, most of which were private, apart from the nursery and show garden.

Gil grabbed her in a bear hug. "Lovely to see you, Avery."

Avery felt flustered, and tried to laugh it off. "Well, it's nice to be wanted. I think." She took a large sip of wine, and a few deep breaths while the new arrivals grabbed drinks from the fridge, and Alex pulled out cheese and pate.

He loaded up a tray and handed it to Avery. "Would you mind?"

"No," she stuttered. "Where do you want it?"

"The coffee table," he directed, and picked up another tray and headed to the living room.

The group trailed after them, Gil and Elspeth sitting on the couch, while the others sat on huge floor cushions. Avery felt a whisper of magic and the lights around the room dimmed, as the fire flared in the fireplace.

"That's better," El said. "I was starting to feel chilly." Her long limbs were crossed beneath her on the couch, and she took a large slug of bottled beer.

Avery realised it really had been a long time since she'd seen them, and she felt suddenly guilty, although she couldn't work out why. She thought of the photo of Gil and again wondered what to do. As if he read her mind, Gil caught her eye and smiled.

"Come on, then," Briar said. "What's going on?"

"Does anything have to be going on?" Alex said. "Can't five witches get together for Friday drinks?"

"Four witches sometimes get together—Avery does not. Therefore, something must have happened."

Alex glanced at Avery. "We've both had a premonition. Enough to merit bringing it to everyone's attention."

"What kind of premonition?" Gil asked, concerned.

"Ladies first," Alex said, winking at her.

Avery tried not to glare at him. "I read the cards and saw that something is coming. Something dark. Something that will threaten us. I read the cards several times and saw the same things—the Tower, Death, the Fool, the Moon, and many sword cards. And then Alex came to see me." She turned to him and found him watching her, his eyes narrowed as he listened. "What about you, Alex? You never said what you saw."

"I was sitting here—well, at the counter, actually," he said, nodding to the long counter that separated the kitchen from the living room. "I was just looking into my coffee thinking about what I had to do that day when I experienced a rush of darkness, almost a blackout, and I saw a man coming. He was dark-haired but faceless, and he brought danger. I could see blood and steel, maybe a blade. And a burning anger and desire. It was so strong, I knocked my cup over and almost scalded myself."

Gil leaned forward, "Did you recognise him? Anything that was familiar?"

"Nothing." Alex was a joker, a tease, but there was nothing light about his mood tonight. "It felt personal, though."

"But what could he want?" El asked. "We have nothing that anyone who knows magic could desire. Nothing unusual, nothing powerful." She looked around the group, perplexed and questioning, "Well, I haven't, anyway."

Avery shook her head slowly. "Me, neither." The others agreed, although Gil looked down at the floor, lost in thought. Avery looked over at Alex. "But how did you know that I would have seen it, too? It was bit odd that you simply arrived at two in the morning."

He hesitated for a moment, and then said, "You, more than any of us—well, other than me—have the gift of sight. As soon as I had my vision, I knew you had sensed something, too. I waited all day to see if the feeling would go, and it didn't. It woke me up and I had to see you, straight away." He shrugged, looking at her with an unusual intimacy, "I can't explain it other than that."

Avery made a decision, and she looked around at the others. "I did find something interesting today, although I don't know if it's anything to do with our premonitions. I was gifted some books by a lady who recently died, and I visited her house today to pick everything up from her son. She had compiled files and family trees on lots of old White Haven families, as well as histories on shops, buildings, and an interesting collection of old town maps. My family tree was in there, as was Alex's. I haven't had chance to go through it all properly yet. " She omitted the part about the photo. "It was a bit spooky, actually, like I was being spied on."

The atmosphere changed, and they all lowered their drinks and leaned forward.

"Who was it?" Alex asked immediately.

"Anne Somersby, she lived on Waverley Road. She was an old lady who was a bit of a local historian. Every now and again she'd come into the shop and look to see what books we had on the area."

"What do you mean, our family histories?" El asked.

"All of us. I haven't gone through everything yet, though."

"What kind of family histories?" Gil asked, his beer on the table forgotten. "I mean, was there anything in mine?"

Was that more than natural concern she heard in his voice? "I haven't had a chance to have a good look, Gil, they look like family trees with a brief bio on some family members. Although, she's done the same to lots of old families in the area. Not just those with the craft."

"Was there any mention of magic?"

"No! None." She again omitted the scent of magic she had discovered.

"What have you done with all the records you've found?" Alex asked.

"They're in my flat, which is sealed and warded, so they're safe."

He nodded, satisfied, but then he surprised her by asking, "The son, is he staying there? At her house?"

She looked at him, confused, "No idea. Why?"

"I think we should check the house out. See if there's more there."

"Are you mad? That's breaking and entering!"

"We won't do any harm! We're just looking."

She couldn't believe she was hearing this, but no one else seemed to be putting up a fight. "No way! What if he's there?"

"Take a look at those papers tomorrow, and then see if you can find where he's staying. I think we should look, but not tonight. We'll wait until you find out more."

El had been watching them both. "Do you think this has to do with your premonition then?"

Avery shrugged. "Maybe. Or it could be some weird, random co-incidence."

Gil shook his head. "We know better than that. There's no such thing as coincidence. It all means something. Maybe she'd found something."

The room fell silent because they knew he was right. The fates moved in odd, unimaginable ways, and just because they couldn't see the cause of something, or see where it led, didn't mean there weren't connections. It was like a web all around them; you just had to know where to look.

Four

The next day the shop was busy and Avery was tired, especially as she hadn't arrived home until late the previous night.

At just after 5:00 PM when the last customer disappeared, she locked up, said goodbye to Sally, and passed through the internal door at the rear that was normally kept locked for privacy, and up the stairs into her flat.

The building that housed her shop and flat was 18th Century, and had originally been three buildings, until years ago when her family had bought them all and converted them into one. The bookshop was on the ground floor, and the next floor contained an open living room, dining room and kitchen, a bathroom, and a spare bedroom. The top floor was in the attic and housed her bedroom and an en suite bathroom, while the rest of the space made up her spell room and workspace.

The spell room was her favourite room in the whole house. The floor was made of polished wooden floorboards, slightly scuffed now, and covered in a variety of colourful old rugs. Two worn leather sofas and an old armchair sat facing each other in the centre of the room, a small table between them. At the far side of the long room were an old oak cupboard, drawers, and a wooden table. Against the walls were shelves packed with books, many old, their pages worn, and all of her magic equipment, including her herbs, tinctures, syrups, and potions.

And it was messy, like most of her house. She accumulated books, objects, pictures, and art, and they spread everywhere in random and haphazard collections.

She walked through the living room and threw open the balcony doors, letting a warm breeze flow through the house. She headed to the kitchen and lit a bundle of herbs to clear her head, and then grabbed a glass of wine.

The boxes she'd inherited from Anne were still spread over the living room floor, so she opened them up to check what was in each, and then started to categorise them, deciding to put all the notes on families and the family trees together, reference books in another pile, and the fiction in another.

The logical place to start would be with the notes on Gil's family. She felt she was prying but it was clearly important, and he hadn't said no. Within the box file was a large family tree that went back generations; the writing was small and immaculate, and must have taken her a long time to create. There were copies of birth certificates, marriages and deaths, and a history of the house, all the way back to the 1500s. She didn't have to go far to find what she was looking for.

Gil was definitely on the family tree, which was at first a relief, until she realised he could still be an imposter. But how would he have fooled his whole family, unless there was the whole 'switched at birth' thing happening? And that would have included his family in the collusion. It was only when she looked closely at the dates of birth of his grandfather and his great-uncle that she realised what Anne's scribbled statement meant. Gil's great-uncle was actually the oldest son, and his children were the true heirs of the Jackson estate. Gil was actually not in the direct line of inheritance.

Avery leaned against the old sofa behind her and the papers dropped onto her lap. Was the family in the photo Gil's great-uncle's family? Were any descendants still alive, and did they know about their thwarted inheritance? She pulled the photo out and looked at it again. It must be them; the photo was of that era, although there was no date or any other identifying notes on it.

She stared at the man in the photo, and a cold chill swept over her. His eyes were dark and compelling, but up close there seemed to be an unflinching gaze staring back at her, offering a challenge. He was younger than she had first assumed, and the children at his feet were toddlers. She checked the family tree again. Gil's great-uncle's name was Addison—a popular name for the oldest male. What was even odder was that there was no date of death recorded next to his name.

Another chill ran through her. He must be dead; he'd be over a hundred by now. Perhaps Anne couldn't find any death certificates. His wife Philippa's date of death wasn't there, either. His children were named, but there was no further history on them at all. No dates of death, or recorded marriages or children. It was as if the whole family had disappeared.

There were several questions that now needed answering. *Did Gil know? How had Anne found the photo? And where was the family now?* And for no discernible reason, the words *black magic* kept pushing to the front of her mind.

Suddenly, the lamps inexplicably switched off, the doors slammed shut, and a wild wind carried around the room, lifting all the papers up and dropping them again. A presence seemed to fill the space, and Avery suppressed the urge to scream. She jumped to her feet and summoning her powers, sent a blast of light outwards from her hands and lit every single light, electric and candles, until the room dazzled with brightness.

The bulb overhead exploded, but the lamps remained on and the candles blazed.

Avery looked around, unnerved, her heart pounding. *What had caused that?* But the darkness had fled and she went to one of the windows overlooking the street to see if she could see anything unusual. It was after seven now, but it was midsummer and still light, and people strolled about heading to pubs and restaurants. Everything looked perfectly normal. Although she hated to admit it, she was seriously disturbed. She needed to have people around her, and despite her reservations, the best person to speak to was Alex.

The premonition was right. Something *was* coming, and she thought it might be connected to Gil.

Avery entered The Wayward Son and made her way to the bar, catching Alex's eye. His eyes widened quickly with surprise and he headed over, a look of concern on his face. "What's happened? You're as white as a sheet."

Avery lowered her voice and leaned in, although with the noise in the pub she doubted anyone could hear. "I don't know, if I'm honest. A weird, supernatural wind flew around my flat when I was looking at Gil's family tree, and I felt something there. A presence. I think I've found something." So close to Alex, she could smell the faint scent of his aftershave and resisted the urge to inhale deeply.

He fell silent for a second and then pulled a menu from the side of the bar. "Are you hungry?"

"Starving, actually." She realised she hadn't eaten since lunch.

"Grab a seat in the back room, and I'll come and take your order. I should be able to join you." He added, "It's on the house."

She frowned. "Don't be ridiculous, I'm happy to pay."

He pushed a glass of wine into her hands. "Just sit and look at the menu! I'll be with you soon."

Avery snaked through the crowded pub to the room at the back she had passed through the previous night. It was quieter here, and a few tables were free. She wondered if Alex had cast a spell to keep it that way. She sat at a small table under the window looking out on the courtyard garden and wearily sipped her wine, trying to shake her mood.

The menu was in front of her, but she gazed outside, thinking about what the incident in the flat could have meant. She ran through various scenarios but kept coming back to black magic, and wondered if someone knew what she had found. Or rather, what Anne had found.

A few minutes later, Alex sat opposite her and plonked a pint of beer on the table. "What you having?" He nodded at the menu.

She picked it up. "I haven't looked. What do you recommend?"

He didn't hesitate. "The steak."

"Sounds good." She pushed her chair back, "I'll go and order."

"No!" He waved her down. "I'll get one, too. Medium rare okay?"

"Fine." She was too tired to argue, and decided that letting him order would be the easiest thing to do. If she was honest, she wasn't sure she should be here telling him anything. She wasn't sure she trusted him.

When he came back, he said, "Go on then. What happened?"

She wasn't sure where to begin. "How well do you know Gil?"

He just looked at her for a few seconds, confused. "As well as you do, I suppose. Why?"

"Do you know anything about his family?"

"Not really, other than they're super rich and he's got a huge house. And a rich magical legacy, obviously." He leaned closer and dropped his voice. "What's this about?"

"Do you trust him?"

"As much as I trust anyone."

"I found a photo in Anne's collection of notes. It was a photo of Gil's home, very old, black and white, and scrawled on the back was a line saying, 'the real Jacksons.' It freaked me out, so I went through Anne's family tree on Gil, and I found that he's not the real heir. He's descended from the second son. His great-uncle Addison's family should have inherited everything."

"Okay, that's slightly weird, but maybe Addison was bad news, or he argued with his parents and was disinherited." Alex looked slightly disappointed. "Is that all?"

Avery persisted. "But there's no death date for either him, his wife, or his kids. That *is* weird. And it was right after I read that, that this hideous wind rolled around my flat and it went really dark. *Something* was in there with me."

"It didn't hurt you?"

"No, I summoned light and blasted the flat with it, but it made me jump. That's not normal."

He shrugged. "We're not normal. But yes, it's weird. And no dates of death?"

Avery shook her head.

"Also weird, but maybe Anne had trouble finding their records." He leaned back in his chair watching her for a few seconds, and then he gazed out of the window, thinking.

"And another thing," Avery added. "There were signs of protection around Anne's house when I went yesterday. Well, at the front door, anyway."

"Is there anything else you've neglected to tell me so far?" Alex asked, a dangerous edge to his voice.

"No!" she shot back. "I don't think so, anyway."

"I may not have been around for a while, but I *am* quite trustworthy, you know!" Alex frowned. "While you're in the mood to share, would you like to tell me exactly why I piss you off so much?"

"You're very sensitive. You don't piss me off." That wasn't strictly true, but she was buggered if she was going to explain.

"Liar," he smirked.

"If the rest of the evening is going to be spent like this, I'll go!" Avery went to push her chair back and felt it locked in position. She glared at him and said in a low, threatening voice, "Release my chair right now!"

"No. Food's coming, and I don't want to eat alone."

One of the bar staff headed over, grinning. "Here you go, two steaks. *Bon appetite*, boss!" He nodded at Alex and left them to it.

At the smell and sight of the food, Avery thought she might die soon if she didn't eat and picked up her knife and fork. "Do you pin all your dates to the chair like this?"

"I didn't think this was a date," he grinned.

"Oh, sod off and let me eat." She cut a large wedge of steak and took a bite.

They fell silent for a few seconds while they ate, and Alex looked deep in thought. "Why don't I help you look tomorrow? We'd work quicker together, and there's safety in numbers."

Before she could answer, her phone rang and she pulled it out of her bag. She frowned at the unknown number. "Sorry, I better get this. Hi, Avery from Happenstance Books. Can I help?"

"Hi Avery, great. It's Paul, Anne's son. I've found something else Anne wanted you to have."

Avery looked up at Alex, and almost stumbled over her words. "Oh, that's great. Is it more books?"

Alex watched her carefully as he continued, and she mouthed at him, *It's Paul.*

"Well, no actually," Paul answered. "I don't think so, anyway. I've found a big box in the attic with your name on it. It's all taped up, so I haven't disturbed it. Do you want to come and get it? Maybe tomorrow?"

"Yes, perfect. What about ten in the morning?" she said, thinking she could do with a small lie in.

"Excellent. See you then." He rang off before she could ask anything else.

"Well?" Alex asked.

"This is getting really weird. Anne's left me something else. A box in her attic with my name on it!"

"Well, I'm coming with you, so you'd better pick me up." He looked at her and grimaced. "Don't argue. It could be a trap. You have no idea who this Paul guy is, or if he knows something."

"If he was going to attack me, he could have done that yesterday. But," she added, seeing his mutinous expression, "I'll pick you up anyway."

"Unless you stay here tonight. It's probably safer."

She shook her head, thinking that staying with Alex would be far too intimate. "No, I'll be fine. The cats will keep me company."

As if he'd read her mind, he said, "I'll be on the couch."

"Yes, you would be!" she said haughtily, "But honestly, I'm okay. Thank you."

He grinned, "Another time, then. In the meantime, have another glass of wine and tell me about this Paul guy and everything you haven't told me so far."

Five

I f Paul was shocked or disappointed to see two of them at his door the next morning, he didn't show it. "Come in! Two of you. Great idea. That box is big and heavy—I couldn't get it down the attic stairs. I've found a few other things, too."

Alex shook his hand. "Nice to meet you, Paul. Lead the way."

Paul led them upstairs and along dusty corridors. The decorating, like downstairs, was old fashioned and floral, and through open doors they could see dusty bedrooms and an outdated bathroom. Both of them were on their guard, but Avery was aware of Alex's solid presence behind her, which was very comforting.

At the end of one corridor was a small door almost hidden in the panelling surrounding it. "They liked to disguise their attic doors years ago," he said by way of explanation. It creaked as he opened it, and they followed him up the bare, wooden steps.

As soon as they reached the attic door, Avery felt the gentle pull of a spell and she glanced around uneasily. The attic was dim and shadowy, lit only by very small windows that at the moment were on the wrong side of the house to catch the morning sun. Paul flicked on the light switch and a single, bare bulb in the middle of the room lit up the space. It was filled with lots of old crap from what Avery could see. Old chairs, broken furniture, and boxes and boxes of stuff. He led them to a box in the far corner.

"Here you go. It wasn't until you'd left on Friday that I read Anne's note again. She'd left me a list of who's to get what in the will,"' he explained, looking harassed. "I have quite a few things to give to others—you know, jewellery and stuff. She said there were a couple of boxes, as well as the books for you, and I had to come searching for them. I wasn't planning to come up here for a while, so it's lucky I read her instructions again."

Avery was barely listening, looking instead at the box, mystified. She had expected an old cardboard box, but this was a big wooden crate, completely sealed. A note was on top of it, with her name on it. She glanced at Alex and then at Paul. "Wow, Paul, that's pretty big. I wasn't expecting that. Are you sure you're happy for me to have it? I mean, you don't know what's in it. It could be valuable."

She could feel Alex glaring at her, but she ignored him. They had to do this right. She didn't want any repercussions. Paul shook his head. "No, it looks battered and decrepit. I'm a little embarrassed to be giving it to you, if I'm honest."

"No problem, I'm happy to take it off your hands. You have enough to clear," she said, smiling. "Did you say you found a few other things?"

"Just this, really," he said, reaching for a small box on the floor. "It has a big chunky key in it. Not sure what that's for, but there you are."

Thanking him, she put the box into her bag, and said to Alex, "Shall we lift together?"

Paul waved her off. "Let the men do it."

"Too right, you follow us down," Alex agreed, but when Paul's back was turned he mouthed at her, *Look around!* He pointed to the herbs hanging above them. It was a hex bag. Desperate to have more time in the attic, Avery whispered a small spell and a loud knock emanated from downstairs.

Paul looked annoyed. "Sorry, I better go and get that, I've got someone else coming to pick up some old furniture. Are you okay to wait?"

"Of course, don't rush," she reassured him. "I'm sure I can help manoeuvre it to the door, at least."

"I'll be back in a minute," he said, and almost ran across the attic and down the stairs.

Alex grinned. "Well improvised!"

"My pleasure," she said, grinning back for a second before becoming serious. "What the hell is in this box, and what's with the herb bundles?"

"If she didn't know magic, she knew someone who did." Alex looked at the box at their feet. "I'm really worried what we're going to find in there." He reached up to the herb bundle and pulled it gently from the ceiling. "Protection again. Quick, let's check out the rest of the room while we have a chance."

They both darted around, searching corners and rafters. Alex called softly from the window. "Another sign of protection."

"I wonder," Avery said, heading to the attic door. She checked the frame inside and out and pulled up some peeling wallpaper along the edge. Beneath it was another rune scratched into the wall above the centre of the frame. "Alex," she hissed. "There's another sign here."

He joined her at the door. "This is too odd. The sooner we look in that box, the better."

"I'm not so sure. I have the horrible feeling we're going to wish Anne had never left me anything."

An hour later they were back at Avery's flat, the box in the centre of the living room. It wasn't as heavy as it looked, but it was bulky and Avery had struggled to lift it, Alex taking more than his share of the weight. After frequent stops they had finally wrestled it up the stairs and they now stood looking at it with worried expressions.

Alex had brought a big crow bar with him from the back of the garage, and he tried to prise under what looked like the lid, but he couldn't get it to move. "There's no edge. It's completely sealed."

Understanding began to dawn. "The spells of protection in the attic have been hiding this box. Could we be seeing something that's been disguised? I mean, it's probably not a crate." Avery ran to the spiral stairs that led up to the attic. "I'll grab my grimoire. I have a few spells that might work."

When she returned, Avery put her spell book on the coffee table, faced the box, and started to recite the most likely spell. Nothing happened, and she flicked through the pages, Alex peering over her shoulder. "I'll try another," she murmured. It was an old spell, a counter-spell, in fact, to dispel veils of illusion. As she uttered the words, strange things began to happen to the box. A mist seemed to rise from it, and Avery's vision blurred and she blinked quickly. The box continued to shimmer until the image of the wooden crate completely disappeared, and instead they saw a sturdy, dark wooden box, carved on all sides with strange symbols. A thick iron band was wrapped around it, and in it was a keyhole.

"Holy crap. That looks sinister," Alex said. "Where the hell did Anne find that, and how did she know to give it to you?"

He was right. The symbols, old runes by the look of them, seemed to impart a warning.

"I'm not sure I even want to open it," Avery said, trying to stop her mouth from gaping open.

"Where's your sense of adventure?" Alex said, dropping to his knees. He ran his fingers over the box, feeling the carvings. "How old do you think this is?"

She shrugged. "I have no idea. Hundreds of years old, probably. I don't do furniture, I do books."

"Gil might know. He likes antiques."

"This might be about Gil's family. Stuff they wouldn't want us to know. And at the moment, I don't know what to think about Gil. I want to trust him, but I don't think we can involve him yet."

"I agree," Alex said. "We keep it between us. We don't even tell Briar or El yet. Come on; let's protect this space before we open it."

She sat on the rug opposite him and he reached his hands out. "I'll lead. There's a spell I think will work well here. Will you let me?"

She nodded and put her hands in his. They were strong and warm and he gripped hers tightly.

"Can you feel anything here?" she asked.

"From yesterday? No, can you?"

"No. Whatever it was has gone."

"You chased it off," he said, squeezing her fingers reassuringly. "Anyway, let me start."

She fell silent as he started to chant. The language was old English, an ancient spell that she was familiar with but had never used. He spoke it well, and power whipped around her quickly, giving her a glowing sureness of protection as it spread across the room. She felt his presence reach across to hers with an unexpected intimacy, and as they connected, the power surged stronger until the room resonated with it like a clear bell. The candles placed about the room sparked into life, chasing shadows from dark corners, and she felt herself relax like she hadn't in days.

"Good. Done." He released her hands and turned to the box. "You should open it. It's gifted to you, after all."

She nodded and pulled the box with the key in it from her leather bag that lay next to her on the floor. Nervous, she fumbled and then slotted the key in the lock. It took several attempts to turn it, until finally the old mechanism clicked and the lock released. She flipped back the heavy bar and lifted the lid, gently resting it back against the coffee table.

A musty, old smell escaped, and glancing at each other nervously they both peered inside. The box was full of magical objects. There was an ancient Athame—a witch's knife used for spells—an old bowl or cauldron, several objects that had been wrapped in paper discoloured with age, and some folded paper. A decayed bundle of herbs in a cotton bag were wedged into a corner.

A tremor of excitement rippled through Avery, and she reached into the box. "This stuff is old. Really old. And it's proper magical stuff."

She pulled out the paper and unfolded it gently, and Alex moved next to her, his arm pressing against hers, so he could look, too. Trying to ignore the tingle it sent through her body, she attempted to read the first few lines.

"It's a letter, or a note."

"From when?" he asked.

She tried to read the writing on the first page. The ink had bled in places, but it was just about legible. *"October 1589. The Witchfinder General is coming to White Haven."*

She felt her breath catch and her fingers trembled, and she looked at Alex in shock. "The witch hunter? Holy crap, Alex. Where has this stuff come from?"

They both knew what had happened when the Witchfinder arrived. Helena Marchmont, Avery's long distant relative, had been burnt at the stake.

"We'll read it later," he nudged her softly. "I have a feeling it will take a while to decipher that writing. I'm wondering if the rest of this stuff is from the same date." He pulled one of the paper-wrapped objects out and as he peeled off the paper it cracked as if in protest. It was a glass jar. "An alembic jar—for potions."

Avery unwrapped another package and found a second jar, this one conical, the glass old with small bubbles in it. "Someone liked potions."

They pulled the other packages out until a range of old glass jars were placed in front of them.

Alex shrugged. "It looks like alchemy to me. Maybe someone was trying to find the secret of immortality."

Avery laughed, "Or was trying to turn lead into gold."

"Both are possible, and anything else. The time fits." Alex shuffled his position slightly, crossing his legs, his weight pushing against her, making her acutely aware of his heat and strength. "We should examine the box. Didn't Anne leave you a note?"

"Yes! Good thinking." Avery realised she'd been so caught up with what was inside the box that she'd forgotten to look at the note. Glad of the excuse to pull away, she knelt forward and pulled the envelope with her name on it from the lid. Inside was a sheet of paper. She read it aloud.

"Dear Avery, I appreciate this will be a shock to you, but I've been aware of your—special skills, shall we call it—since you were little. Don't worry, your secret was safe with me.

"White Haven is a magical place, and for years I've been guarding and researching its rich heritage. I was once friends with Gil's grandmother, Lottie, and it was she who revealed the secrets of the old families to me. She knew I would treasure their memory and protect it. And I've protected it well. It was Lottie who taught me simple spells of protection, and Lottie who inscribed the signs around my house. I'm not one of you. She revealed these secrets to me, and asked me to be Guardian, because she knew no one would suspect me, and if anyone came looking for these things, and the other things that are still hidden, there would be no greater protection.

"However, I'm dying. I need to return these things to you and the other families. There's no one I can speak of this to. My son does not know, by the way. He is merely the messenger.

"I'm not a fool, Avery. These things have been hidden for a reason. Witchcraft is both light and dark. Lottie's own uncle was banished from the house for his persistence in black magic, his name stricken from the family records. I'm not sure Gil knows of this. But Lottie always feared he would be back. He or his descendants. He was searching for the old grimoires. The originals. You must find them first. Lottie says the spells they contain are

powerful. When the witch hunter arrived, they were hidden for everyone's sake. When Helena Marchmont was burnt at the stake, the others fled, fearing if she wasn't safe, then no one was. It was only years later that the families returned here, and as you know, some never stay long.

"I have done what I can to help you in my small way, but Lottie didn't know, and I certainly haven't discovered, where those grimoires are. I've researched the town and the family histories—yours, Alex's, Gil's, Elspeth's, and Briar's—but I couldn't find what happened to Gil's great-uncle Addison. It was as if he simply vanished.

"I wish you luck my dear. I think you'll need it.

Yours, Anne Somersby."

A chill rushed through Avery's body and she felt everything shift, as if her life had suddenly changed in ways she couldn't yet comprehend. She looked at Alex. "Did you know about any of this? The missing grimoires, the banished brother?"

He rolled his eyes. "Are you mad? How could I possibly know! That's what a secret is, you muppet." He grabbed the letter and skimmed it again.

"I'm not a muppet!" she said, outraged.

"So then don't ask stupid questions."

Despite Avery's annoyance with Alex about all sorts of things, mainly for just being Alex, she realised she was incredibly grateful that he was here with her now. She ran her hands through her hair. "Sorry. I'm feeling nervous."

"I know." He grinned, "That's why you have me here. To protect you. It's my pleasure."

"You are so annoying."

"So are you," he said, and rose to his feet, stretching.

She ignored him. "We're going to have to let the others know. I guess this leaves Gil in the clear."

Alex nodded. "I think so. We need to find out about these other grimoires. If I'm honest, I'm not surprised." He stood at the window, looking out onto the street and then looked back at her. "The date on our family grimoire is from 1790. What about yours?"

She shuffled over to look at the front of her grimoire, and saw the date scribbled at the top, the long list of witches' names beneath it, Avery's being the latest. "1795."

"Well over two centuries after the witch trials swept the country." He looked at the boxes strewn about the room. "If Anne's done a good job, there'll be lots in there to help us."

Avery nodded, resoluteness now pouring through her. "So, someone's coming. For us and the grimoires—wherever they are. We need to prepare. You better get your magic on, Alex."

Six

After contacting the others to come around later, Alex spent the afternoon helping Avery carry everything she picked up from Anne's house into the attic so they'd have more room to spread out. It would also mean other casual visitors to the flat would have no idea what they'd found.

He looked at her living room, perplexed and amused. "Do you normally have so much stuff around?"

Avery looked at the stacks of books, magazines, and the clothing strewn around the room and wondered what he was talking about. She liked ethnic everything, and there were candles, wall hangings, and throws strewn across the couch, as well as large, bright kilim rugs on the wooden floor. Her books and magazines were strategically placed next to favourite spots, and houseplants were everywhere. Yes, it was slightly chaotic, but she loved it. It was warm and comfortable—her nest. "Er, yes. I like it lived in."

"Congratulations. It certainly looks it." He smiled at her, one eyebrow raised, and Avery felt a flush of colour on her cheeks. *Was he insulting her house?*

"What's wrong with it?" she retorted.

"Nothing! It's not a criticism," he said, still grinning at her in his infuriating manner. He gestured at her, an all-encompassing sweep of his hand that travelled from her head to her toes, and she looked down at her long dress and back at him. He continued, "It's an observation. It's very you. I like it."

She narrowed her eyes at him, wondering quite how to take his last comment, and decided it was better left ignored.

When they'd finished moving everything, they collapsed on the attic floor, both of them hot and sweaty. Alex lay sprawled on the rug in a patch of late afternoon sunshine, like a cat basking in the heat, while Avery leaned against the sofa looking at the carved wooden box as if it would explode.

"What are you thinking?" Alex asked, still prone and eyes closed. "I can hear your mind whirring away from here."

"I'm wondering what that note says."

He rolled to his side and propped himself up on his elbow, fixing her with his dark brown eyes. "Well, we've got a couple of hours before the others get here. Why don't we read it? Or rather, you read it, and I'll listen."

"Do you think we should wait for the others?"

"No, it'll probably take ages to decipher that spidery writing."

"Good. I was hoping you'd say that." She leaned across him to reach into the box, trying not to touch him while all the while remembering the flash of well-toned abs she'd seen when he'd carried the boxes up the stairs.

She was aware of him watching her and she tried to ignore him as she swiftly grabbed the papers and leaned back against the sofa. He grinned at her and leaned back again, closing his eyes. "Have at it!" he said dramatically.

Unseen, Avery rolled her eyes. There were only a handful of pages, and she turned them over gently, scared she'd damage them, as the paper crackled beneath her fingers. "I'm really nervous. What if we find out something terrible?"

"It's a million years ago, Ave," he said, shortening her name in an unexpected intimacy. She quite liked it and watched him speculatively, feeling like a peeping tom because he couldn't see her. His long limbs were muscular and strong, and his jeans hugged his thighs in all the right ways. One hand was under his head, the other rested on his very flat stomach. She dragged her eyes away and back to the diary.

"But whoever's written this letter could be one of our ancestors."

"Yes they could, probably Gil's, but it's not going to read itself!"

"All right!" Slowly and hesitantly she started to read. She said the first line again and felt her stomach lurch.

> *"October 1589. The Witchfinder General is coming to White Haven.*

> *"We have been lucky here in White Haven. We are far from the cities and have remained quiet and in- sular, those of us who practice the craft able to keep our magic a secret. But a sickness is sweeping the country. The rumours swirl and thicken and we hear that the Witchfinder General is coming—only days away. He has stopped in small towns along the way and we hear of interrogations and public shaming, drowning, and even a burning at the stake. But they are not real witch- es, not as we are.*

> *"We cannot run and start again elsewhere, it is too obvious. And besides, there are other things to consider,*

things that will have long term implications. We have decided we must hide our books and practices, bury them deep before he arrives, before he burns us all. Our magic is not as powerful as it once was - for reasons I cannot explain here, but to use it in front of everyone will endanger not only our children, but the whole town. All our grimoires will be hidden about White Haven and our properties. We must decide where, swiftly.

"I choose to hide these tools beneath his very eyes, and he will not see them. These items are covered with wards and seals. The others think I am mad, but I am confident of my own magic. He will not find these objects, although the book I will put elsewhere.

"I am hopeful that he will leave town without finding anything, and then in a few months I can reclaim what is mine, and my family's heritage. But if not... I cannot shake this fear that something will go wrong and that we will all die before any of them can be found. We prepare for the future, however. Our magic will not die. It will course through the veins of our children — it is our legacy. But it is this fear that causes me to write this note — just in case. I see things others don't, and I see the long, dark shadow of the Witchfinder General and I see blood and fire. I tell myself it is my imagination, but that is to deny my power.

"If someone else finds this note then I am dead, but I hope it will not be too late to find the book. I believe I have hidden it wisely. Our book has old spells from the dark times, and our power of spirit and fire. Whoever you are, when you choose to look for it, think of what we do. It will be there. And then guard it well.

Imogen Bonneville."

Alex shot upright, looking at Avery in shock. "Did you say, 'Bonneville?'"

She swallowed, "Yes."

"But that's *my* surname."

"I know. I did warn you it might be one of our ancestors!"

His dark eyes were troubled, and he stretched his hand out and took the note. "I know, but thinking it and knowing it are two very different things."

Avery leaned back, watching him and thinking. "At least one of your ancestors wasn't burnt at the stake." She shuddered. "I know it happened a long time ago, but it suddenly feels like it happened only last year. It's one of those things I push to the back of my mind. I still can't believe Helena didn't use her powers to escape."

"It would put everyone at risk, the letter said as much. Can you imagine if that happened now?"

"There must have been more to it than that. She said, '*Our magic is not as powerful as it once was.*' And I don't want to think about that happening again. We may have to use our magic more openly if we get threatened, and then what?"

"I'm not sure we can afford to do that now, any more than they could then." Alex looked at the note. "Imogen mentions a prophecy, and a legacy of fire, so they are clearly skills that run in my family. But how did this box end up at Gil's house?"

"Another mystery to add to the many," Avery observed, thinking that life was about to get far more complicated, and probably dangerous.

Briar, El, and Gil looked at them both in amazement. The box sat in the middle of the attic floor in pride of place, the rest of the files and books surrounding it, spread on the floor in all directions. They perched on floor cushions, rugs, and the sagging sofas. Candles filled the room, and the scent of incense drifted around.

"So, you found this box in Anne's attic?" Gil asked, again.

"Yes. I know it's weird, but she's been hiding it for years," Avery explained for what seemed the hundredth time. "And she got it from your great-aunt."

"But it actually belongs to me," Alex added.

Gil closed his eyes and leaned back on the sofa. "I need time to think."

"But Gil," Briar said insistently, "you really had no idea about your crazy, black magic-seeking uncle?"

"Great-great-uncle," he murmured without opening his eyes. "No! I did not."

"And what about your brother?" she asked, referring to Reuben, Gil's younger brother who generally avoided all magic.

"I doubt he knows, either." He remained prone on the sofa, hands over his eyes.

Alex interrupted, "Briar, can we give Gil a moment without the twenty questions?"

Briar looked at him wide-eyed. "They're important questions, Alex. Some crazy person from his family is after some old hidden grimoires, and we are at risk!"

"Yes, thank you, Briar, I know that. But this is not the time for blame. It's not Gil's fault. And actually, we don't know what we sense yet. It could be Gil's family, or it could be someone completely different."

Avery suppressed a smile, enjoying the fact that Briar was at the receiving end of Alex's sarcasm and not her. If she was honest, Briar was a little brittle tonight. As soon as she'd arrived at Avery's flat, she looked around suspiciously, and narrowed her eyes when she saw Alex already there, leaning against the kitchen counter with a beer in hand. *Did she fancy Alex?* Avery wouldn't be surprised. He was very good looking, she had to admit. He had that rugged self-assuredness that was infuriating but mesmerising all at the same time. She found his closeness surprisingly unsettling.

Avery tucked a strand of her dark red hair behind her ear and coughed slightly. "So, to get back to our plan. We need to go through all of this paperwork and see if we can work out where the old grimoires are."

El spoke for the first time in ages, "And see what else our old histories may show us."

"Exactly," Avery looked at El gratefully. "We also need to look at the old town plans, records, and anything else. And we need to work quickly, before someone else works it out before us."

"How come none of us knew about the old grimoires?" Briar asked. "Surely family members would have passed them down."

"Oh, I can tell you why." Gil sat up and rubbed his hair so that it spiked upwards. "Fear. After Helena died, I would imagine they were only too happy to let them disappear completely."

"But the grimoires are our strength," Avery reasoned. "Surely when the risk was over, at least one family would have gone back for theirs."

El shrugged. "Another mystery. And what about the box? Have you examined it?"

"Every inch," Alex said. "I recognise some symbols, but not all. Runes are not really my speciality. It's a bit weird that it may have been carved by or for my family."

El shuffled forward and sat next to the box, her silver bangles jangling as she ran her hands across the surface. "It must be several centuries old, right?" She looked up at them, "And we think these objects are from the 1500s?"

"We think so, yes," Alex confirmed. "If we use the letter to date it."

"I'm familiar with runes, and these ones offer protection. They ward off evil, and hide it from prying eyes."

"If they could do this, why didn't they do it with the grimoires?" Briar asked.

"Still too big a risk, I would imagine," Avery said. "Anyway, I've started looking through the history of the town. Do you know where your old family houses would have been?"

"Well, you know where mine is," Gil said. "We haven't moved in years. I would imagine our grimoire is hidden within the grounds, but maybe I'm being simplistic."

"Well, it sounds like your great-great uncle Addison had been looking for it, and he must have looked everywhere," Alex reasoned. He looked at Gil, puzzled. "Did you really have no idea about him and your disappeared line?"

"No, none." Gil looked at them, still raking his hand through his hair. "I'm in shock, actually. I'll have to speak to Reu about it, but I'm sure he knows nothing, either. As you know, he prefers to ignore our magic."

Avery didn't really know Reuben, but he was closer to her age, and very different to Gil. "Are you sure he doesn't like magic, Gil? I would have thought he would have moved from White Haven if he wanted to ignore his history. Like my sister did." Sometimes magic didn't run strongly in all family members, and sometimes they just preferred to ignore it and bury their talent. Her sister, Bryony, had buried it for years and moved away, unlike Avery who had honed and practised her magic, becoming stronger every day. The thought of finding the old family grimoire filled her with excitement.

"I don't know what he thinks, Avery, we just don't talk about it anymore."

"How does it work with your wife, Gil?" Briar asked. She sat cross-legged on a cushion, watchful, and it seemed to Avery, still annoyed about something. "Does she know about your magic? I mean, I presume she does, but…"

"I hide it," he said. "All of it."

Avery felt a jolt of disbelief, and looked at him, shocked. Gil was the only one of them who was married, or in fact in a relationship of any kind. It wasn't that any of them hadn't been in relationships, but they didn't last that long. She presumed for his marriage to have lasted, his wife, Alicia, must have known.

"Really?" Alex also seemed surprised. "How is that even possible? You live with her every day. Aren't you hiding part of yourself? Your real self?"

Gil thought for a moment. "I've broached the subject, you know, of the history of this place, and what would she think if there really were witches, but she looked at me like I was mad." He looked at the others, a rueful smile on his face. "I left it, and kept promising myself I'd bring it up later, but chickened out." He looked at them all and laughed. "You should see your faces! I know it's mad, but I've made it work." He became serious, dropping his gaze to the floor for a second, before looking up sheepishly. "I was lonely, and I needed her. I *need* her now. I don't know how you do it. We're so different from everyone else, I just needed a connection."

El, Avery, Alex, and Briar looked at each other, a flash of under-standing passing between them.

"It's all right, mate," Alex said awkwardly. "You don't need to ex-plain yourself to us."

El smiled sadly, and leaned against the wooden box. "I envy you, Gil. It is hard, that's why I came back here. It's why I like hanging out with your brother. He might not practice magic, but at least he understands it. And me."

Avery tried to hide her surprise. Elspeth, like Briar, had moved back to White Haven a few years ago. Their families had moved away when they were children, and both had felt White Haven's magical pull, returning in their early twenties. She had no idea El spent time with Reuben, and realised there were so many connections she didn't know about.

Gil obviously knew, because he just nodded. "I know. I'm hoping you'll change his mind."

El shook her head. "I think it would take something big to do that."

"Well," Briar said, looking regretful, "My last boyfriend loved that I could make all these cool potions and creams, except when he suspected they might really work. He just couldn't get his head around it, no matter how much I tried to play it down. It was the midnight herb gathering that really freaked him out. The whole relationship thing exhausts me. Unless I meet someone who understands me, I've sworn off it for the future." She glanced at Alex and then stared into distance, lost in thought.

"And what about you, Avery?" Alex asked.

His stare was so direct; it felt intimate, even with everyone else there, and Avery stumbled over her words. "I guess I've had the same experience as everyone else. Old boyfriends have thought I was odd, with endearing hobbies—you know, my tarot reading and book obsessions—and I really played them down. I thought my last boyfriend was okay with it, but it turns out, he wasn't. But lucky me, we remain good friends!" She shrugged, feeling embarrassed, even though there was no need to. "And what about you, Alex?" she asked, returning the question. "No secret girlfriends hidden away?"

He laughed. "Several, all at arm's length."

"No surprises there, then," Avery said, rolling her eyes as everyone laughed.

"Liar," El said, unexpectedly, watching Alex with her head tucked speculatively on one side. "You don't fool me, Alex Bonneville. That ladies man thing is just an act."

Alex's response was just as unexpected. He threw his head back and laughed. "No comment. I reserve the right to privacy. As do my women. And there's always room for more." He winked at El, Briar, and Avery.

"You're revolting!" Briar shrieked in mock horror, and threw a cushion at Alex, who laughed again.

Gil tried to bring them back to order. "If we can move on from Alex's harem, what's the plan with these grimoires?"

Avery answered, trying to shake off the memory of the glint in Alex's eye. He was way too dangerously sexy. And unobtainable. Instead she voiced something she didn't really believe, but thought she'd say anyway. "Maybe we should leave these grimoires alone. To find them could change everything. We've managed all these years without them."

"It's too late for that," Alex said. "I think that the moment Anne Somersby died, something was set in motion. And we both know something else is coming," he said, looking pointedly at Avery. "We have no choice, we have to find the grimoires first, and whatever else is hidden from our past. And we have to stick together."

"I can't take any of this home yet," Gil said. "Do you mind if I leave it here?"

"No, of course not," Avery said, shrugging. "Where do you hide your grimoire at home, though?"

He grinned. "There's a hidden room in the attic. But I rarely go up there. The spells I need for my garden I know by heart. Alicia just thinks I have eccentric gardening habits. She doesn't like gardening, anyway, and her job keeps her busy."

"Well, I don't want to move this box, not in the daylight, anyway," Alex said. "If that's okay, Avery? I'll take the files, though. Exciting bedtime reading!"

"Sure, whatever you want."

El agreed. "I'll take my family papers, too, but all the general stuff on the town and that, maybe we should leave here?"

"I agree," Briar added. "Let's meet again, soon. Share what we have."

Avery nodded, "All right, Wednesday night?"

"What are we all doing for the Solstice?" Alex asked. "That's only a week away. We should celebrate it together."

Avery had never celebrated it with anyone else before, but before she could protest, a chorus of agreement rang out. Alex grinned, a triumphant smile as he glanced at Avery. "Good, I'll start planning."

Seven

When she wasn't working at the shop, Avery spent every spare moment in the attic looking at her family tree and piecing the history of her family together, while also reading up on White Haven's history. Anne had really done her research, and Avery's head swam with details.

She had a meticulous family tree, going back to the 1500s. Whether Anne couldn't find anything before then, or had given up at that point, it wasn't clear. She'd also glanced at Gil's, and that went back to the 1500s, too. It must have taken Anne years. It was odd, to spend so much time on someone else's history. Some of the names on her family tree coincided with names written in the front of her grimoire. She remembered adding her own when she was sixteen, her mother encouraging her in the family traditions. The only time she had, actually. Shortly after that her mother left White Haven, and she hadn't revealed anything about a previous spell book, lost or otherwise. Maybe she didn't know about it.

Amongst Anne's papers was a map of White Haven and the surrounding area, marked with numbers and letters, and Avery pinned it to the wall, removing a few prints to make room. She marked Gil's house on there. It was the only one that they knew had belonged to the family through the years. But where had everyone else's family once lived? She was pretty sure that the bookshop and the house it was in only belonged to the family in the late 1800s.

It was a couple of evenings after their discovery, and Avery lifted her head from her research and looked around at the attic, wondering about the other witches who had stood there working their spells. It was cluttered with papers and books from Anne, her own spell book, and books on herbs, metals, and gems. Her tarot cards were on the table, folded in silk and placed in their own special box. The carved wooden box still sat on the floor, although she had pushed it to the side, under the window. It drew her eye all the time, no matter where in the room she sat.

As the light faded and the shadows lengthened across the floor, Avery felt unsettled and restless. She grabbed a bundle of sage from the shelf and lit the end with a flash from her fingers. The sage sizzled and smoked, and she marched to a corner of the room, chanting a cleansing spell as she worked around the room, clearing the air.

With another click of her fingers, she lit the candles, and the dark corners pooled with a warm yellow light, immediately comforting her. She sat and pulled out her tarot cards, shuffling them thoroughly and focusing on what she wanted to ask them. Alex's image came to her mind, but she pushed it away. She wanted to know if something was still coming. A stranger, a threat, or what?

The pack warmed beneath her hands and she slowed her breathing as she started to place out the cards. As she turned each one, she saw representations of herself, Alex, and a card that could be Gil, and then the major arcana cards came, chilling her blood. The Devil, the Tower, and the Moon, and too many sword cards, ending with the King of Swords.

She swept the cards up in a hurry, jumping when she heard a knock on the door. Attackers didn't usually knock, she reassured herself, as she ran down the two flights of stairs to her front door. She could see Alex's silhouette through the glass and she felt relieved, if puzzled. She opened the door and he stepped in, grinning and waving a bottle of wine. He looked good tonight, his long hair loose and freshly washed; he smelt of something musky.

"I come bearing gifts!" He hesitated as he looked at her. "Are you all right?"

"I'm fine, I've just read the cards again and they look awful. You made me jump, that's all."

"Well, good job I'm here then. Do you mind if I look at that box again?"

"Of course not, it's yours."

He looked at her expectantly. "Glasses?"

She grinned. "Carry on up, I'll grab them."

By the time she returned to the attic, Alex had dragged the box to the centre of the room again, and now sat cross-legged in front of it, examining it closely. He had pulled a book from his canvas pack and it lay open next to him, revealing pages illustrated with drawings and descriptions of runes.

Avery sat next to him and picked up the book. "Where did you get this from?"

"El. She's had it for years and has marked a couple she thought looked familiar." He pointed to one on the side of the box. "This one is for protection and repels demons." He looked at her with a raised eyebrow.

"Demons? As in, red-eyed, evil smoke and brimstone demons?"

"I guess so." He pointed to the opposite side, where another strange mark was carved into the wood. "And this one repels spirits." He pulled the book from her hands and flicked through a few pages. "See, here."

Avery compared the two, and felt a flutter of excitement start to override her fear. "And the one on the top?"

"Incomprehension, blindness—a deflection, almost, of vision. The one that stopped us from seeing the box." He leaned closer, looking at the details. "See, there are lots of tiny little runes, too, all around the rim of the lid of the box."

The lid was deep and solid, with more runes on the inside. "And what do these mean?" she asked, pointing at them.

"Another spell." Alex's voice rose slightly with anticipation. "They combine to make a sentence." He looked back and forth between the runes and the box, flicking pages impatiently, muttering under his breath.

While he looked, Avery ran her fingers over the runes, feeling their smooth contours. She had the feeling they hadn't been carved by hand, but had been magicked in, burnt by fire. *Should they even be trying to open it?* She sat back on her heels, thinking. It was deep enough to hold a grimoire. Maybe Imogen Bonneville had been lying in her letter. She felt a thrill race through her. If this did contain the grimoire, they were ahead of whatever was coming.

"Alex, I think the grimoire is in the lid."

"What?" he said absently, still pre-occupied.

"Your family grimoire. The original."

He looked up at her in shock. "But the note..."

"Meant to confuse—I think so, anyway."

He looked back to the pages in front of him. "Okay. This makes sense. I think I know what the runes say. It requires a blood sacrifice."

"What!" Avery jolted back. "We don't do those." They never did such things. That was darker, older magic, now forbidden.

"Hold on—it's not what you think. It needs my blood." He may have said the words calmly, but he looked worried.

"Go on." She took a slug of wine, trying to ease her racing thoughts, and Alex reached for his glass, too.

"It needs something of me, something to prove who I am, and that I am worthy of it."

The room felt very dark suddenly, and Avery shivered. "Your ancestor surely wouldn't want to cause you harm?"

"I think it's also an act of faith."

"There's a lot of *thinks* here." As much as Alex annoyed her, she didn't want him dead or maimed. And she didn't relish the thought of black magic unleashed in her home.

"Will you help me?" She hesitated, and he carried on. "I had another vision. More blood, more destruction. I see death, Avery."

"What if it's this?"

"It's not this. This will help us."

"The cards I saw earlier predicted it, too. Destruction, I mean. Change." Her well-ordered life, weird as it may be to some people, was also safe, and now it felt threatened. She sighed. "We can't walk away from this now, can we?"

He shook his head, his long dark hair falling round his face, and in the candlelight she became aware of just how attracted to him she was. He had an animal magnetism, a sheer masculine force that she couldn't ignore, but really had to. She was pretty sure he wasn't interested in her at all, and if he was, she was only one among many. And, she reminded herself, he was a superior bastard at times.

"It's a simple spell; it just requires some herbs and my blood. I don't actually need you to do anything, just be here in case something crap happens." He grinned and winked.

"That's not funny. I'm not the witch cavalry. Should we call the others?" With the night closing in around them, her attic felt threatened and vulnerable. More witches were a good idea.

"No, it would take too long. Let's get on with it," he said decisively, rising quickly to his feet. He headed to her extensive collection of dried herbs and selected some jars, declaring, "I need this, this, and this."

While he was preparing the herbs by crushing them in the pestle and mortar, she flicked through the rune book, looking at the designs and comparing them to the box. "Are you sure you know what you're doing? I'm familiar with a couple of these, but…" Her voice trailed off as she tried to work out the meaning.

"My grandmother was good with runes," he said from where he stood at the long wooden table. "She taught me some, a long time ago. I remember a few of them now—vaguely. I must have her books somewhere, or maybe she took them with her."

"Where's your grandmother now?"

"Not here," he said with a sigh. Before she could ask anything else, he brought the herb mix over. "Now, I just have to mix my blood in it."

"We need a black candle," Avery said. "It will enhance the spell, discover the truth of it, and banish negative energies." She headed to the shelf to where a number of baskets sat, and after rummaging in one of them, she pulled out a brand new candle, while Alex marked out a circle on the floor with salt.

"Salt?" She looked at him, confused.

"I'm taking precautions. Just in case something unhealthy appears." He shrugged. "I'm sure it won't."

She resisted the urge to glare. "In that case, we need purple candles, too."

Alex placed the box in the centre of the circle, and then Avery lit the candles on either side.

He looked at her, serious all of a sudden. "Ready?"

"As I'll ever be."

"Step away, just in case."

He waited until she was across the room, standing by the table, and then he stepped into the circle and sat cross-legged in front of the box, withdrew a penknife, and slashed it along the centre of his palm. Avery winced as she watched him. He clenched his hand and let the blood drip into the bowl, all the while chanting under his breath. He mixed the blood and herbs with his uninjured hand and started to smear the mixture over the runes in the lid and the tiny ones all the way around the edge. All the while his blood dripped into the bowl, and he seemed to smear a lot of it over the box.

As Alex chanted, the pressure dropped, and Avery realised she was having difficulty breathing. She started gasping for breath, and noticed Alex was doing the same, but she daren't speak. Something, good or ill, was happening. With a weird sucking sound the pressure dropped again, and Avery felt dizzy as every single candle in the room went out, and then the lamps, until only the two candles in the circle remained lit.

Avery concentrated on Alex and the box. Long, wavering shadows made him look demonic, and it looked as if the runes on the box were moving.

Just as the pain in her ears was becoming unbearable, there was a loud bang like a gunshot, and the wooden lid of the box cracked down the middle. Thick, black smoke began to pour from it. The candle flames on either side of the box shrank to tiny sparks, and Alex chanted louder, lifting his head to stare at the smoke.

Avery stepped forward, raising her hands, ready to send a blast of energy at whatever it was, but the thick smoke stopped within the circle's protective walls. She remembered Alex's words. *He said it was a test, but was it?* The signs on the box provided protection from spirits and demons. Maybe something was locked in.

She stood transfixed. Alex's voice was strained and he was enveloped in the blackness, almost shouting his chant. She stepped forward again, wondering what else she could do, when suddenly the blackness crackled like it contained lightning and disappeared, leaving Alex slumped on the floor. The candle flames on either side shot high before shrinking again, and the pressure in the room returned to normal.

Whatever it was, had gone.

Avery used her pent up energy to relight every single candle and ran to Alex, pulling him out of the circle, until she fell over backwards on the rug, with him sprawled on her lap.

She eyed the box warily, but nothing else happened, and she quickly felt Alex's neck for a pulse. She sighed with relief. It was there, strong and steady, but he was a dead weight and completely unconscious.

She leaned over him awkwardly, and shook his shoulders. "Alex, Alex, can you hear me?"

Nothing.

She shouted louder, "Alex. Wake up!"

She had a sudden, horrific thought that he might be possessed, and then chastised herself. *This wasn't Supernatural. But could it happen?* She and the others used the elements, did spells of protection, but they never messed with blood magic. Well, never until now. *What the hell had they got themselves into?*

She looked at his inert form. He was really heavy. And solid. His arms were sinewy with muscle, his shoulders broad, and his shirt had rolled up as she dragged him over, revealing a smooth flat stomach. Her gaze travelled down his legs, and she swallowed guiltily. Tearing her eyes away she focused on his face and shouted again, "Alex, wake up!"

Still nothing.

She glanced at the box and decided she needed to complete the salt circle again. She felt vulnerable and open to attack, having no idea what had been in the black smoke. Sliding out from under Alex, she rested his head gently on a cushion and scooted over to the box, all her senses alert, as she peered into the crack in the wooden lid. She could see a hint of silver. *Something* was in there, but she'd leave it for Alex to look. She grabbed the salt and completed the circle once more.

Avery was tempted to wake him using a spell, but decided against it. He must have used up a lot of energy, and only rest would restore that. His hand was still bleeding from the cut he'd made across his palm, so she fetched a bandage from the bathroom and dressed the wound. Then she angled a pillow under his head, and threw a blanket over him, trying to make him as comfortable as possible.

The room felt chilly now, even though it was summer. There was a small fireplace in the wall between her bedroom and the attached en suite bathroom, and the rest of the attic space, as the main chimney breast rose between what had once been two separate houses. She lit a small fire, the bright orange of the flames making her feel warmer already.

She wondered how the others were getting on with their research. The past had always felt close to her, and now it felt even closer. She had the feeling that old secrets were ready to be uncovered, whether she wanted them to be or not. Shivering, she pulled a blanket around her shoulders and lay on the sofa, a cushion under her head. It wasn't long before she slept, too.

Eight

When Avery woke the next morning, she found Alex gone and his blanket draped over her. He'd left a note on the table.

I didn't want to disturb you, so I'll see you tonight. The others will be coming, too. Don't touch the box until we arrive. Thanks for your help. I'm all right.

- Alex

Of course, it was Wednesday. She looked around the room, expecting to see the room disturbed in some way after the events of the previous night, but in the pale dawn light, everything looked fine, apart from the broken lid of the wooden box. She felt sorry Alex had left; she would have loved to know what he'd experienced, but that would have to wait.

After showering and applying makeup, she pulled on a long cotton skirt in dark blue and a short-sleeved cotton top before she headed downstairs to the shop. The day was overcast and promised rain, and that was usually good for visitors. On Wednesdays, only she and Sally were in the shop, which kept them busy. On other days, a post-grad student named Dan would come in for a few hours, which relieved Avery from needing to be in the shop all day. She didn't like leaving Sally on her own.

Sally grinned at her when she arrived. "What have you been up to? You look like you had a late night."

"Nothing that exciting," Avery lied. She'd already decided on how she would explain seeing more of the others. It would be unusual enough for Sally to comment. "You know when Anne Somersby left us some books?"

"Yes," Sally said, leaning her hip against the shop counter.

"She left me some papers on some old family histories and the history of the town. They include Alex's, Gil's, and a few others—you know Elspeth from the jewellery shop, and Briar with the lotion store?"

"Yes." Sally drew the word out quizzically, a slight frown behind her eyes.

"Well, I let them know, and we've decided to finish her investigations," she said lightly, while making herself busy tidying shelves. "Alex came over last night and it ended up being a late night, that's all. They're back this evening."

Sally's voice went up an octave. "What do you mean, 'came over?' Are you two—?"

Avery leapt in before she could finish the sentence, whipping round to face Sally. "No! It was just a chat."

"A late night chat." Sally smiled smugly. "Call it what you want to, I'll make a cuppa," and she disappeared into the back room.

Avery sighed and rested her head against the bookshelf. This would now go on and on. She hoped customers would keep them busy all day.

By the time they closed the shop, Avery was knackered. They had been busy all day, so she hadn't had time to worry about other things. She locked up and headed upstairs to her flat.

El arrived first, looking excited. "Hey Avery, that stuff you gave me from Anne is great." She rested a big, slouchy leather bag on the floor, bulging with papers. Her white-blonde hair was scraped up in a messy bun on her head, and she wore faded jeans and a t-shirt, revealing a glimpse of the tattoos on her upper arms. "I've found out so much more about my old family history than my family ever told me."

"Who gave you your grimoire then, El?" Avery asked, curious.

"My great aunt. And she was sneaky about it, too. Made me promise not to tell my parents, or anyone else in the family. Magic was a big no-no to them."

Avery was in the open kitchen area, preparing tea and coffee. "So how did she know that you would be okay with it?"

"She noticed things that the rest of my family either couldn't see, or didn't want to. I was always clever with making things, and she noticed that I made things slightly differently. She made a point of visiting as I was growing up, and then one day she asked me if I wanted to spend the weekend at her house. It was a creaky old place, but over the course of that weekend she told me about our family, as much as she knew anyway, and she started to teach me magic. After that, it was our little secret." Elspeth smiled and shrugged. "She was amazing. It if wasn't for her, I may not even be here."

Avery passed her a mug of coffee. "I guess I've been lucky. At least it wasn't something to be hidden in our family. Not from each other, anyway. Although not all family members have embraced it."

"Strange, isn't it, how some people are scared of this stuff?" Elspeth laughed, "And then a whole load of other people wish they had what we have."

"I don't know if they'd want what we have now. Things got weird last night."

Before she could elaborate, the others arrived. Alex looked tired.

"Are you okay?" Avery asked. "You really worried me last night."

"What's going on?" Briar asked, a look of concern crossing her face as she looked between the two of them.

"It's all right, I'm fine," Alex said. "Sorry I didn't stay," he said to Avery. "I woke at about three in the morning and didn't want to wake you, so I left. Are you all right?"

"I wasn't the one smothered in weird black smoke. I'm fine, thanks. Weirded out, but fine."

By now the others were looking bewildered, and Alex quickly said, "The runes on the box, it was a test, for me. Come and see."

They followed him up the stairs to the attic, which looked peaceful, if messy, suggesting nothing of the events that happened the night before. The wooden box rested in a patch of sunlight, highlighting the crack on the inside of the lid. The line of salt still surrounded it.

"What the hell happened?" Gil asked. "Is that *blood*?" He stood close to the box, examining the smear of herb paste that ran over the runes, and the bowl the paste had been mixed in. Alex's knife was still on the floor, too, and he looked at Alex's bandaged hand. He straightened up, suddenly serious. "What did you do?"

"The box needed my blood to prove who I was. Or rather, my ancestor did. It was a rune spell, and I deciphered it."

"And then decided to cast it! Blood magic?" Gil looked at Alex incredulously, and then at Avery. "And you let him do it?"

Avery had never seen Gil like this before. She knew Gil as the laid-back witch from across the town who came from one of the old families. But then again, they'd never performed magic together, either.

She stood next to Alex, in solidarity. "I actually didn't want him to, but we knew something was in the lid. It's still in the lid. We think it's the grimoire." The tension in the room was palpable. "Look, I know it was dangerous, but we were careful, you can see that. And I trusted Alex." She felt Alex give her a quick glance, but she kept looking at Gil.

Gil's shoulders dropped and he sighed. "I wish you'd have called us first. Anything could have happened."

Alex explained, "There wasn't time, and besides, I didn't think we needed you. And I'm fine."

"And the black smoke?" El asked, hands on hips, not wanting to let them off that easily.

He grinned sheepishly, "Well, that *was* odd."

"It wasn't smoke though, was it?" Briar said, standing next to the circle. "It was a spirit form."

Avery's mouth gaped. "It was a *what*?"

"She's right," Alex said. "It spoke to me. Well, sort of. I could feel it in my head, probing, checking me out." He shook his head, as if to shake out the intrusion. "I felt I had to fight to prove who I am. It was exhausting."

"You passed out. It must have been," Avery said, frowning at Alex. "I didn't know whether to try and intervene, but then I thought if you're right, and it was a test ..." She trailed off, and looked at Briar. "It was crazy. Anything could have happened, but we had to try. How do you know it was a spirit?"

Briar gently probed around the crack on the box's lid, and then brushed her fingers across the symbol on the side. "This sign. It seems logical now."

"Well, hindsight's a great thing. You could have been killed. Both of you," Gil said, still annoyed. He sat on the edge of the sofa, looking at the box warily.

Alex strode forward to join Briar. "Well, we weren't, and it's about time we looked at what's in here."

He inserted his fingers into the long crack in the lid and pulled, the fractured wood splintering to reveal a large, thick grimoire covered with scuffed black leather. Alex lifted it out gently and as the light hit it, a faded silver image glinted on the cover that Avery struggled to recognise. Alex carried it to the oak table that Avery used to prepare her spells, and they crowded around him as he opened the cover. A list of names was written on the front page in different scripts, and the date at the top said 1309.

"This was 300 years old when it was hidden!" he said, shocked. He turned the pages, and it seemed everyone held their breath. The pages were covered in dense, tiny writing, all spells starting on a new page, the same as in their existing grimoires, the language old, and the script hard to decipher. There were simple illustrations too.

"What kind of spells are they?" El asked, craning to see.

"Some of them seem the usual types," Alex said thoughtfully. "Charms of protection, healing spells, some curses, and ..." He paused, looking at them, "Spells to control spirits and demons."

"Demons?" Briar asked, her eyes wide.

He nodded. "Many more than I've got in my existing book."

Avery felt another flutter of worry pass through her. She had been taught as a child that to manipulate spirits and demons was something that could be done only occasionally - it was too dangerous. "Does this mean they summoned demons more than we do now?"

"I guess so." Alex continued to turn pages, mesmerised. "These spells are sophisticated, complex. And potentially more powerful than I've used before."

It took a few seconds for this to sink in. Older, more powerful spells. A hidden legacy of magic they could now learn. Avery shivered, not sure if it was with excitement or trepidation. "Do you think the other grimoires will be like this?"

"They must be," Gil reasoned. "Is there anything in there about immortality? Or anything that looks particularly dark?"

"Other than *demons*? No idea at this stage." Alex looked up. "I really need to spend time looking through this properly. The writing's hard to decipher in places."

"Why are you asking that?" El asked Gil.

"Just wondered if it's something my missing relatives might have been interested in."

Briar interrupted, looking horrified. "Has anybody actually summoned a demon?"

"Never," El said. "And I have no intention of doing so either."

"I wonder," Avery said, "If it was Anne's death that triggered something coming in the first place. I mean that her death released knowledge of the box she'd hidden away for so long. After all, it was just after she died that Alex had his premonition and the cards foretold an event."

"Alex," El mused thoughtfully, "what are the main types of spells in your book?"

"I'm not sure, it's difficult to define. Astral projection, out of body walking, spirit talking." He was sitting now, head on his hand, leafing through the book, his attention completely caught in it. "I've never seen stuff like this before."

"So it's a symbol for Spirit!" she exclaimed. "The image on the front of the book, I mean."

Avery was annoyed with herself for not realising sooner. "Of course! And it *is* Alex's strength."

"So does that mean the other grimoires focus on the other elements?" Gil asked.

"Fire, Air, Water, Earth. The strengths of our family lines?" Briar observed.

Avery grinned. "We could grow our magic! Learn new things. Tap into a magic that's been hidden to us for centuries!"

Gil brought her back to Earth. "If the spells are as powerful as we think—as Alex thinks his are—then the books could be trouble. A whole shit ton of trouble. If someone else knows these exist, it's no wonder they're coming for them."

Nine

The following morning, Avery was up and out early. The streets and lanes of White Haven were quiet, and wisps of early morning mist started to clear as the sun rose into a pale blue sky.

Avery walked up the hill away from her flat and Happenstance Books, and at the top looked back over the town and the sea beyond. She never tired of this beautiful view. She loved the old cobbled streets and tiny lanes that snaked into each other as they rose and fell with the land, finally leading down to the sea. Fishing boats were heading out, but the sailboats remained in the harbour, their bright sails furled. Beyond the town, the houses were spaced out along the hills and fields. It was such a pretty place, and she wanted it to remain that way. She didn't want a witch war breaking out in White Haven in the search for old grimoires.

Last night, once the other witches had gone, she'd made herself a chamomile tea and shut the door between her bedroom and the attic. She sat in bed with the lights low and the window open, and spread Anne's papers across the duvet. Her cats, Circe and Medea, had curled up on the end of the bed, keeping her company, ears pricked, eyes closed, while she'd scrutinised old maps of the town. And that's when she saw Anne's mark on the page, a small green-inked squiggle that looked like an 'H.' *Could that be for Helena?*

That spot was where she was heading this morning.

Avery turned from the view and headed along the lanes until she found the one she needed. Besom Lane. It wasn't somewhere you would pass by chance. It was tucked out of the way, and lined with tiny cottages. She meandered along it, admiring the hanging baskets and pots, the neat curtains and whitewashed walls, and carefully noted the numbers. The lane was long and winding, and she eventually arrived at the cottage she was looking for.

This tiny place could have been where Helena and her family lived all those years ago. There was a window downstairs next to the front door, and two small windows upstairs, the cottage identical to the others on either side. It was strange to think she had lived so close to this place and had never known to whom it had once belonged.

Avery leaned back against the wall of the house opposite and gazed at it, her thoughts jumbled. *Was Helena dragged from here to the stake, or was she already imprisoned somewhere in the village?* She looked again at the map. It was fuzzy and unclear compared to modern maps, and although Anne had noted a number, for all Avery knew, the numbers might have changed over the years. The map showed small square gardens at the back, and this row was almost buried in the slope of the hill behind it. But whereas the lanes were isolated back then, now they were surrounded by streets lined with more recent buildings—well, 18th century as opposed to 16th century.

What now? Would the old grimoire be hidden here? Avery wracked her brain trying to think about what Anne's note had said. The cottage must have withstood many changes and renovations; it would be a miracle if they found it here. She sighed. It was time for coffee and breakfast. She'd go and see who else might be awake.

Avery pushed open the door to Briar's shop, the door chimes ringing pleasantly as she entered. She carried two hot lattes in a cardboard tray, and a bag of croissants was wedged into the top of her shoulder bag.

As soon she entered the shop the scents of lavender, rose, and geranium wrapped around her. She inhaled deeply and looked around with pleasure. Briar's shop looked like an old fashioned apothecary. Shelves lined the walls, filled with different ranges of skin lotions, hair products, soaps, creams for ailments, and all sorts of dried herbs, books on herbs, scented candles, and other products used around the home. All of them were made with natural ingredients, either by Briar or other small companies. You could tell which were Briar's products, because they were all in unusually shaped bottles with pale pastel colours. It was a comforting shop, and Avery immediately relaxed.

Briar looked up from behind the long wooden counter at the back of the shop and smiled, puzzled. "Hi, Avery! Is everything all right? I don't normally see you in here." She'd been filling some jars with a creamy lotion that looked like moisturiser, and she finished her work, putting the jug on the counter.

"Don't let me stop you! Yes, I'm fine—sort of. I've bought coffee and croissants so I can pick your brain." She plonked her bag and the rest of her load on the counter. "Your shop looks great!"

Briar smiled. "Thanks. I've been doing well, so I expanded my range." She grinned and leaned forward, grabbing a coffee. "People often comment on the unexpected benefits of using my stuff."

Avery laughed. "I bet! If they only knew."

"Probably best they don't." Briar sipped her coffee. "This is good, thank you." She dipped the croissant in and took a bite. "Even better!" She watched Avery as she chewed. "So, what are you picking my brain about?"

Avery looked around to make sure the shop was still empty. "Old grimoires, of course. I'm worried we'll never find the others."

"Well, if we don't, maybe someone else can't find them, either. It might be a good thing, from what we saw in Alex's book."

"Do you really think that? It's our heritage!"

Briar licked her fingers. "It's been five hundred years since we've seen those books, and our magic has survived. It's brought us a good life." She gestured to the room around her. "We've never needed them before, and we don't need them now." Briar looked calm and composed, and very resolute.

"Does this mean you're not going to look for your book? Or where you used to live?" Avery felt herself floundering. "Or anything?"

"I don't know. We have a lot to lose."

"We have a lot to gain, as well. And someone's coming."

Briar sighed and rolled her eyes. "But who? I mean, really? This is just too weird. Anne dies, you and Alex are seeing the same stuff. All of this hidden information is suddenly revealed. It feels like a set-up. I'm not sure this stuff should be found."

"But Alex already has his. The box. The grimoire. The message from Imogen, his ancestor. From Gil's." Avery appealed to Briar, feeling she needed to make her see sense. "I thought you were excited about the news?"

"I was, and now I'm not so sure." Briar started to fill her jars again, the smell of geranium wafting between them. "I have a bad feeling about this. I don't like dark magic, and I won't do it."

"I don't, either. And we don't know if this is dark magic. It could be about harnessing untapped potential."

Briar shook her head, the long dark curls framing her pretty face. "I'll see how the rest of you get on. Until then my papers about my family tree and my place in White Haven remain locked away."

Avery was suddenly disappointed, and then curious. "How did you end up here, Briar? El was telling me that her great-aunt told her—it was their secret."

Briar nodded. "I know, she told me that, too. For me it was different. I found out through letters."

"Letters?" That certainly wasn't the answer Avery was expecting.

"Yes. Sent by my parents to each other, debating back and forth as to whether they should tell me or not." Avery must have looked baffled, because she smiled. "My father travelled a lot for his work, and he and my mother wrote to each other all the time. There was an incident at school—I had a rush of magic and did something that freaked a few in the class out. I can't even remember what now, nothing major. My mother told me I was special and hinted at powers, and then she said nothing else. A few years later my dad died in an accident, and a few years after that, so did she. That's when I found the letters. The conversations were veiled, but I understood enough to know what they were referring to. They wanted to shield me. So I came here, to the place they used to call home."

"How did you learn to use your magic, then? It would have been hard if no one taught you."

"I taught myself. Although they had given up the life of magic, they couldn't bear to part with everything. Or, my mother couldn't. I found lots of books and the family grimoire. And then I came here and met all of you, and Elspeth has taught me lots. So has Gil."

Avery's mouth fell open in shock. She had no idea that Briar had been such a novice when she arrived, or that the others had helped so much. And then she felt incredibly guilty. "I didn't realise. I'm so sorry; I should have helped you, too."

Briar shrugged. "It's okay, Avery, you've always done your own thing. You like it, I don't. I need the others."

Lately Avery had started to wonder how true that was, but she turned the conversation back to Briar. "But you've learnt so much. You're brilliant. A natural!"

Briar smiled ruefully. "I don't know about that."

Avery shook her head, feeling a rush of annoyance. "Briar, I'm confused. You could learn so much about your past now. And yet, you're turning your back on it!"

"It's complicated. I feel I'm only just getting to grips with things, and now this happens. I move at a different pace than you."

Avery felt bereft all of a sudden, and frustrated. She was only just starting to understand Briar. "Will you still come to the Solstice celebration?"

Briar smiled. "Of course. I'm still a witch."

Ten

A very's next stop was El's jewellery shop. She wanted to reassure herself that El wasn't having second thoughts, either. As much as she was trying very hard to respect Briar's annoyingly sensible decision, she was annoyed with her for being so, well, *annoyingly sensible.* Really, was this the time to have second thoughts, when old magic and new powers were so close?

The closer she got to El's place, the crosser she became.

El's shop was close to the seafront, down one of the lanes that ran off from the quayside. The strong smell of brine oozed around her as she arrived outside. The shop front was a big window made up of small square bevelled panes that made the interior hard to see, especially because a display was set up under the window, showing necklaces and earrings in unusual designs, as well as a collection of decorated knives.

Once inside, Avery found that El's shop was much darker than Briar's, and smaller. The walls were lined with dark-patterned wallpaper, and the display cases were lined with black velvet. The lighting was low, and fairy lights were placed around the displays. High above the counter at the back of the shop was a selection of knives and swords. They looked wickedly sharp, as well as ornamental. On the far side of the shop was a collection of metal bowls and objects used in witchcraft. El had clearly decided to market herself as Wiccan, and a strong smell of sandalwood incense swirled around the shop.

She had to push through a group of girls who were admiring the jewellery, holding earrings against their ears in front of a mirror. A young woman stood behind the glass-topped counter that was used to display more jewellery.

Avery introduced herself. "Hi, I'm a friend of El's. Do you know where she is?"

The young woman had black hair cut into a blunt bob, the ends died purple, and she wore a tight black dress that showed every curve. Her face was pale but expertly made up, her lips painted a blood red. In comparison, Avery felt underdressed. As usual, her long red hair was loose and she wore one of her ankle-length flowing dresses with flip-flops. She felt like a wild woman in front of this groomed creature, and she had a sudden longing to send a wind whipping through the shop to ruffle her immaculate hair.

The woman gave Avery a quick appraising glance and called back over her shoulder through a partially open door behind the counter. "El! You have a visitor. Some red-haired chick."

Avery grinned. *Chick!* She hadn't been called that in while.

She heard El shout back, "Is that you, Avery?"

"Yes!"

"Come on in."

Without saying a word, the woman gave Avery another long look, and then lifted up the hatch at the end of the counter, allowing Avery to walk through. A practitioner of magic, Avery could tell. She had a quality of knowing. It was unmistakable.

Not bothering to speak either, Avery went into the back room, which was painted a dark red instead of black, and almost stopped in shock. El wasn't alone. Reuben was there, lounging in a chair next to glass doors that opened out into a tiny courtyard. And great Goddess, he was seriously hot.

El grinned. "How are you, Ave? You've met Reuben, haven't you?"

"I'm not sure I have, actually. I've seen you around, of course. I know your brother better." *Was she gabbling?* She felt heat starting on her cheeks, and she hoped she wasn't blushing.

Reuben nodded, "I know. And no, we've never met." He jumped to his feet and extended his hand, and she was surprised by his height. She'd never been so close to him before. He was tall, with an athletic muscular build, very tanned, with tousled blonde hair that had been bleached by the sun. He wore a sleeveless top that had seen better days, and it showed his strong muscular arms, which were covered with a half-sleeve of tattoos. He was wearing board shorts and he had the smell of salt and sea about him. It looked like he'd been surfing. She shook his hand; it was warm and firm and he grinned a gleaming smile. She hoped she wasn't going to giggle like a schoolgirl.

"Want some coffee?" El offered, interrupting her train of thought and providing a welcome distraction as Reuben dropped back into the chair, his long legs stretched out in front of him. El was standing next to a wooden counter than ran under a window overlooking the courtyard. Her hair was piled on the top of her head, and she wore pale blue jeans and a skinny grey tee. Next to her, a collection of jewellery and gems were laid out, and it looked as if she had been working.

"Why not? Tachycardia never hurt anyone."

"What?" El said, confused.

"I've had a lot of coffee today."

El looked at her watch. "Already? It's only ten!"

"Long story." She looked at Reuben, wondering how much to share.

"It's okay," El reassured her as she poured a cup of coffee from a percolator on the bench and passed it over. "He knows everything."

"Oh." For a few seconds, Avery wasn't sure what to say. As far she knew, Reuben wanted nothing to do with witchcraft.

"Your secrets are safe with me," he said, looking amused.

"It's not that," Avery explained, leaning against a cupboard at the back of the room. "I just thought you weren't interested."

"Interested, just not a practitioner."

"I wanted to know what he thought of the whole, weird thing," El explained.

"And?" Avery asked him.

"It sounds dangerous. But intriguing." He shrugged, non-committal, his bright blue eyes assessing her.

"Well, Briar thinks it sounds too weird. She's not doing anything for now," Avery said, trying to keep the annoyance out of her voice and failing. "I wondered if you'd had second thoughts, too, El?"

"No way. Reuben's gonna help me hunt for my grimoire. I think I know where to look." She frowned. "Seriously, Briar's not looking?"

She rolled her eyes. "Not yet. And wait a minute—you know where to look already?" Avery had a rush of relief that El was still in, and then a rush of panic as she realised she didn't have a clue where to look for her own.

"It's just a theory," El continued. "According to Anne's paperwork, my family lived up on the hills above the town. The old crofter cottage—Hawk House."

Avery knew the one she meant immediately. "That was yours? But it's a wreck now."

El grinned. "Exactly. We can check it out without interruptions."
"When?"

"Tonight. No time like the present. You look like a small kid, Avery. Do you want to come?"

"Yes, please! I presume you mean tonight, in the dark?" She faltered for a second, wondering just how creepy that might be.

Reuben smiled a slow sarky grin. "Scared, Avery?"

She narrowed her eyes at him, hating to be called out. "No! I'm coming. Just tell me when."

Avery's final visit of the day was to Alex. If she'd had time she'd have visited Gil, but his house was on the edge of town, and she really should get back to the shop. Sally would think she'd been kidnapped. In fact, she should call her. She pulled her phone from the depths of her bag and saw she'd missed half a dozen calls. *Crap.* She'd left her phone on silent. She guiltily called her, bracing herself.

Sally's voice rang out in her ear. "Are you okay?" She sounded grumpy.

"Of course—I'm fine. I've been catching up with a few things, and honestly didn't think I'd be this long."

"Bloody hell, I wish you'd have left a note. I've been calling you all bloody morning."

"I know. I'm sorry."

"The shop is really freaking busy."

"Sorry, really sorry. I'll be back by lunch." She checked her watch. *Hopefully.* She was right next to The Wayward Son now.

She heard Sally exhale loudly. "Dan's here early, so you can take your time. It's a good thing someone answers their phone."

Avery bit down a reply. She employed Sally; she should chill the hell out. But Sally was her friend and a fantastic manager. Without her, the shop would be a disaster. She adopted her most conciliatory tone. "I'm really sorry. I'll see you soon. Thank Dan for me."

She headed into the pub, deciding she had to buy cake before she headed back. Something to appease her staff. The smells of the kitchen hit her as soon as she entered, and the place already looked busy. The lunchtime rush had started early. She saw Simon, one of the bar staff she remembered from the other night, and she leaned on the bar as he came over, wondering if it was too early to get a pint. It was a quick decision. "Pint of Doom, please."

"Sure." He grabbed a glass and started pouring her drink.

"Alex not working today?"

Simon nodded his head, up towards the ceiling. "Up there. Said he's doing some stuff."

She took her pint and paid. "Cheers."

Avery headed to the back room and went up the stairs, hoping Alex wouldn't mind her dropping in. She knocked and shouted, "Alex, it's me! Avery."

She heard the thump of footsteps and then the door flew open. Alex looked half asleep, his long hair tangled, his stubble darker and thicker than usual. He leaned on the frame, yawning, and then he grinned. "Avery!" He stepped back. "Come in. You'll have to excuse the mess. I was up half the night."

"Bloody hell, Alex. This place *is* a mess. It's worse than mine!"

The room was gloomy, the blinds still down and semi-closed. Papers were strewn across the rug in front of the fireplace almost covering it completely. Half-drunk coffee cups were placed randomly around the room, and a selection of empty beer bottles sat on the kitchen counter. A large corkboard was propped on the floor, leaning against the kitchen workbench, scraps of paper pinned to it.

He pushed his hair back, and then opened the blinds in the kitchen, allowing sunshine to stream in. He squinted for a second, letting his eyes adjust. Even looking half awake, he was still very hot. She had a sudden vision of waking up next to him and wondered what he'd look like naked. Reuben was good looking, but Alex had a smouldering sexiness that she just couldn't ignore. What was the matter with her this morning? She hoped his psychic abilities meant he didn't read minds.

He put the kettle on and called over, "Do you want a coffee?"

She looked guiltily at her pint. "Er, I'm drinking."

He looked at her pint and then at his cup. "That's a way better idea." He pulled a beer from the fridge and popped it open. "Cheers." He took a long slug.

"So, I guess you were researching all night?" Avery looked around the room. "Where's your grimoire?"

"Under that pile of papers." He nodded towards the rug in front of the sofa. He grinned again, dispelling the tiredness. "You should see what's in there, Avery. Hold on, let me get it."

He padded barefoot over to the grimoire, and unearthing it from beneath the papers, he carried it to the kitchen workbench that separated the two rooms.

Seeing it again gave Avery a shock. She had forgotten how much older it was than their existing grimoires. It oozed age and arcane knowledge, the cover guarding long forgotten spells and secrets. She turned the pages, admiring the old script and the drawings in the margins. She was itching to find her own. She looked up to find Alex watching her.

He smiled. "It's beautiful, isn't it?"

She nodded. "Now that you've had a good look at it, what spells have you found?"

He excitedly turned pages, trying to be gentle. "I don't know how this has kept so well, but it's in really good condition. I presume it was the spell on the wooden box. I doubt they knew how long it would have to be hidden for."

Avery frowned. "I doubt the intention was more than a few years. Or even months. Helena's death must have had far-reaching consequences."

"The families fled. Her death would have been catastrophic. Unbelievable, even." He sighed. "It depresses me to think about it. Can you imagine that happening here? Now—to us? Anyway. Spells. Let me show you this." He found the page he was looking for. At the top was an image of linked bodies. Beneath, written in tiny script, was a list of ingredients and a spell.

"What's this?" Avery asked.

"Spirit walking."

"What?"

Alex laughed. "Another word for astral projection. But with someone. What do you think?"

Avery was confused. "Well, I thought that's something you could do, so why do you need a spell?"

"Because I've never done it this way. Or with someone. Shall we?"

Avery looked at his dark eyes, all traces of sleep in them gone. Her heart was beating incredibly fast; he was so close. She had an overwhelming urge to kiss him, but instead said, "Are you insane? You want to spirit walk with me?"

"If you've never done it before then it will be a safe way for you to do it. I'll help you, protect you." He winked, his gaze falling on her lips before he met her eyes again. "I can't think of anyone else I'd rather spirit walk with."

Avery's stomach lurched. *Was Alex flirting with her?* It would be so easy to be seduced by him, and she wasn't completely sure that would be a good thing. "Really? I'm not entirely sure I trust you that much. I thought spirit walking was dangerous."

"Only if you don't know what you're doing. And I do." He was still smirking at her in his insufferable way. "Go on. You know you want to."

As much as she had the feeling she should run in the opposite direction, she really wanted to see what spirit walking was like. "All right. What do I have to do?"

He grinned. "You have to come back here later tonight, when you're already tired. I'll prep the spell and we go from there."

"But I've promised to help El and Reuben search for El's grimoire tonight." She wasn't sure if she was relieved or not.

"Great! El has a plan. And help from Reuben—interesting. How come?"

"I've no idea. He was there at her shop. Looked pretty comfortable, too. Said something about being interested in magic, but not practising it," Avery explained, but thought she'd keep the fact that he looked very hot to herself.

Alex nodded. "Where are they looking?"

"The old Hawk House, up on the downs above the town. It seems it once belonged to her family."

Alex thought for a brief moment, and then decided, "They don't need your help. Not the physical kind, anyway. I'll text her that we'll help in other ways."

"What other ways?"

"Astral ways," he said, grinning.

Eleven

The rest of Avery's day passed in a blur, and all too soon she was back in Alex's flat, her heart pounding uncomfortably, her mouth dry. She leaned against his door before opening it, wondering briefly if she'd gone mad, and why she thought to touch up her make-up before arriving. She wished she were heading to the downs instead.

Before she even knocked, the door flew open, and Alex ushered her in, saying, "Your nervous energy preceded you. I could sense you a mile off."

"Exaggerator," she said, pushing past him.

He locked the door behind her. "We really don't want to get interrupted."

His flat was completely transformed. All traces of the mess from earlier had gone. Despite the warm night, the fire was on low, and the room glittered with candles. In front of the fire was a soft warm blanket, big enough for two. There was no other lighting in the room, and the rich smell of incense drifted around. Avery could feel her mouth dropping open in surprise, and Alex laughed.

"It's easy to get cold when you're lying still, so we need the fire, and we need to be comfortable. The lights help induce a relaxed state."

Right now, Avery thought she would never relax. "I bet that's what you say to all the girls," she shot back, thinking her heartbeat must be audible.

Alex just laughed again, and led her to the rug. The grimoire was on the coffee table behind them, a selection of coloured candles next to it, as well as Alex's Athame and a silver goblet filled with a dark, murky liquid.

"We need to create the protective circle, then take that drink—it will help us enter the right state and help us link, and then we say the spell."

"What's in the drink?" Avery asked, eyeing the concoction warily.

"Valerian, clary sage, vervain, amber, gold leaf, lavender, and bay. And a couple more."

"All right, if you're sure you're not going to poison us."

"Trust me, Ave, I'm a pro."

She resisted the urge to comment, and instead joined him as he used the Athame to create the protective circle by drawing in the air and on the floor. She followed him, lighting the candles and placing them on the four points of the compass. He sat in the middle of the rug, and she sat opposite him, legs crossed, knee to knee. The soft yellow candlelight gave everything a warm glow, and despite herself, she relaxed.

"Do you feel okay?" Alex asked.

"Surprisingly, I do."

"Good."

He took her hands in his, closed his eyes, and took a few deep breaths. Avery did the same, willing her heart to slow as she dropped her shoulders. After a few seconds, he squeezed and released her hands and she opened her eyes to see him holding the small, engraved silver goblet with the liquid inside. He took a few sips and grimaced, and then handed it to her. Avery took a few sips, too and shuddered. It was horrible. Bitter, with a slightly burnt taste to it. She handed it back to Alex and he placed it on the edge of the circle, and then he lay down on his back facing east, and she lay next to him. He took her hand in his and squeezed it again. "Ready?"

"Ready."

Alex started to recite the spell and she closed her eyes again, feeling the energy in the circle change, and her awareness heighten. As he chanted, her breaths deepened and her body relaxed, her limbs becoming heavy. Within seconds she heard Alex's voice in her head, but instead of jolting her awake, it intensified her experience and she embraced his voice. It was like a soft blanket wrapping around her and she wanted to hug it close. As if he could sense it, his presence encompassed her and she responded again, the intimacy almost overwhelming. And then she could see him, his entire form lying a few feet above her. But it wasn't his physical form. He was a pale, silvery blue and he smiled down at her.

"Come on Avery. Join me."

He took her hands and pulled gently and with a *whoosh*, she felt herself sliding up and out of her body until she floated next to him. For a second, a wave of panic washed over her, and then Alex's presence wrapped around her again, calming and reassuring her.

"I'm okay," she said. She saw her physical form lying beneath her, and a long, thin silver cord connecting her spirit to her body, and the same with Alex next to her. "This is so weird," she thought, forgetting Alex could hear her.

"But great, isn't it?" His eyes glowed with a pale light, and as if sensing her discomfort, he said, "Let's just move around the room so you can get used to the feeling. Just move slowly."

He floated away from his body and pulled her with him. The room was dim and shadowy, its colours drained, the candles bright points in the darkness. A powerful purple aura emanated from the grimoire. "Look," she pointed.

Alex nodded. "Magical energy. Very strong, too."

As she followed him, she felt stronger and safer. This was actually fun.

"If you feel worried at any point," he said, "just envision yourself lying here, and follow the cord back to your body."

She nodded as her eyes followed the cord spooling across the room. "Can we go outside?"

"If you feel ready."

"Yes!" She grinned. "This is awesome."

Avery again felt Alex's essence squeeze her own gently, and she responded as he laughed. "This is so cool—way better than doing it on your own. For now I'm going to keep hold of your hand, is that okay?"

"Yes, I'd prefer that."

"Great. This is going to be odd, but don't panic."

He turned and pulled her towards the wall and then through it. She was aware of the strange sensation of brick and stone and then she was free and the stars floated above her. She gasped. "Look!"

Avery rolled onto her back as if she was swimming, and watched the stars glowing in swirls of incandescent light. They looked bigger than she was used to, and the rest of the town below her was pale in comparison. She could see waves of energy flowing around everything. Beyond the pub, she could see the sea, and the immense force of the waves as they rolled in and out further along the beach. The raw power on display was amazing—it was so tangible.

"This is what you draw on, Avery. Do you see it?" Alex asked, his hand the one warm constant in this sea of change around her.

"I do. I feel as if I could touch it." She gasped again as people spilled out from the pub below them. "Look, I can see their auras." The people were dim, but their auras glowed white, or purple, or orange.

"It's easy to see auras here," Alex said. "You'll find it becomes easier when you return to your physical form, too. How're your energy levels?"

"I feel fine. Great, even!"

"Good, let's head up to the downs."

"Can we go that far?" Avery asked, worried.

"Your cord will travel a long way, as long as your energy is good," Alex explained with another squeeze of reassurance. "Come on."

Alex pulled Avery up higher and away across the town to where it became dark, the lights and the people disappearing behind them. In the distance she could see dark purple clouds washing up from where the surf pounded at the cliffs heading out of town. And then she saw the ruined house on the moors, tucked into a curve of hillside, and the pale blue auras of two figures poking around amongst the ruins. Elspeth and Rueben. There was a flare of light along the foundation; it seemed El was using magic.

"She must be using some kind of locator spell," Alex said. "Can you see the lines beneath the earth?"

For a second, Avery couldn't understand what he meant, and then she saw the silvery lines growing stronger by the second, marking the foundation of the old house, some stretching further back up the hill. "Did El do that?"

"She must have. Can they see it, though? Look," Alex gestured further up the hill. A slab of silvered earth glowed for a few seconds, and as they drifted over it, it disappeared.

Avery felt of rush of excitement. "Is that where the book is?"

But before he answered, she felt another wave of energy hit her, but different this time. It felt dark, angry. She tensed and looked up at the same time as Alex. A dark red glow was heading towards them, and

Alex quickly pulled her to his side as a figure became clear ahead of them.

"What the hell is that?" Avery asked, panic racing through her.

"Another spirit walker," Alex said, "and he doesn't mean well."

The figure raced towards them and a wall of power pulsed outwards. Almost simultaneously, Avery sensed Alex push something like a force field towards the approaching figure. The two met with a clash, and although Avery couldn't hear anything, she felt an almost tidal surge of electricity rush around them.

Now was not the time to panic, and Avery stayed close to Alex, doing as he did and summoning her own powers. She was a witch—if she could do this in her physical body, she could do it now.

Alex was totally focussed on their attacker, but she felt him anchoring her, and she joined her force to his, strengthening the shield he had created. Their attacker's form was blurry, non-human, and it was impossible to make out what he or she was. One thing was certain. It was trying to hurt them. The figure pushed closer, trying to crack the protective shield that glowed a pale blue ahead of them. Avery didn't ask what would happen if it broke.

"We need to withdraw, Alex. I don't know what I can do to help."

"To withdraw we have to push it back, to give us time. We do not want it following us back."

"Will it hurt Reuben and El?"

"No, it can only watch. I hope. Listen, we must push together. Let it think it's overpowering us, and then push. Hopefully it will be enough to throw it off balance. And I have a trick up my sleeve."

Avery was vaguely aware of the scene below. The two witches were continuing to work the spell, following the lines beneath the earth, but Alex pulled her attention back.

"We need to protect them, too, give them privacy." He grinned at her, his teeth glowing with a silvery light, his eyes sparkling. "Follow my lead."

The dark mass ahead was pushing against them. Its anger was palpable. Avery felt Alex's energy pull back, and she matched him, allowing their attacker to come closer. She saw two red eyes glowering malevolently, and she felt its premature wave of pleasure at their perceived weakness. They allowed it to creep closer and closer, until Avery was worried it may be too close to repel. Red waves flared like fire around the shield, licking like flames trying to crack their defences.

Alex whispered, "Nearly time. Wait. Wait. *Now*!"

He pushed suddenly, striking out in one massive hit, and Avery joined it, amazed at the strength they created together. Into the middle of it Alex projected a strike like lightning—a silvery bolt that crackled with searing heat. It punctured out through their shield and into their attacker's, sending it shooting backwards.

They barely had time to enjoy their victory when Alex pulled her away, and she did as he told her earlier. She thought of her physical body next to the fire and followed her cord back, racing along it in a blur, Alex next to her. Their attacker was a long way behind them.

Avery returned to her physical body with a *thump*. Her limbs felt heavy, but her mind was alert in an instant and she tried to sit up. A searing pain exploded in her head and she cried out, falling back.

She heard Alex. "It's okay, take your time. You've used a lot of power."

She turned to him, blinking, and the room focussed. The warm orange light was soothing, and the fire still crackled, bathing them in heat. Alex was lying on his side, head propped on one hand, watching her. She took a few deep breaths and felt the pain recede quickly.

"Better?" His voice was a balm to her senses. It almost replaced losing his warm presence that had wrapped around her earlier.

"I think so." She shivered, despite the warmth. "Shouldn't we be doing something? Like joining El and Reuben?"

His close proximity made her nervous, but her gaze wandered from his dark eyes, across his delicious stubble, down to his full lips.

"In a minute," he said softly. And then he leaned forward and kissed her, gently at first.

A flare of desire raced through Avery and she leaned into his kiss. Within seconds his hand was on her back, pulling her close, until she felt his whole body pressed against hers. Her hand snaked around his waist, feeling his muscular build and his warmth. His kisses deepened, and she felt herself falling away, losing herself completely in him.

He eventually pulled away, gazing at her. "I suppose we should go and check on El and Reuben now." But he didn't move, waiting for her response, his gaze still travelling from her eyes to her lips and back again. His hair fell around his face, grazing her cheeks, and his scent enveloped her.

She felt breathless and giddy and wanted nothing more than to stay right there. "I suppose we should."

He grinned, and she melted a little more. "In another minute." And he kissed her again, all playfulness gone as she arched into him, drawing him closer. When they broke apart again, both were breathless.

Avery pushed him away, her hand against his chest. It took every ounce of her willpower. "You're a very bad influence, Alex Bonneville. Our friends could be in trouble."

He reluctantly pulled away. "Come on, then. I'll drive." He pulled her to her feet, and while he grabbed his keys, she extinguished the candles with a word.

Twelve

The narrow lanes were as black as pitch; only the car's headlamps lit the way ahead, giving Alex and Avery brief flashes of hedges, gates, and fields.

"I didn't think a spirit walker could physically attack someone," Avery said. She peered through the windscreen, trying to see if she could see anything in the sky overhead.

"They can't, normally." Alex drove quickly, his eyes on the road. His car was a classic Alfa Romeo Spider, Boat Tail, and it whipped through the country lanes. "I expect El and Reuben will be fine, but I don't know what attacked us. I'm not even sure it was human."

Avery felt a heaviness settle into her body as she thought of demons, ghosts, and other creatures of the night. "What could it be?"

"Either someone wielding dark magic, or a demon."

There. The word was out now.

"But they don't exist." Her voice sounded tinny and weak. She looked at Alex's profile as he concentrated on the road, willing him to agree with her.

"We both know they do." He flicked her a glance. "We just haven't encountered one before."

"Necromancy was very popular hundreds of years ago. Do you think our ancestors summoned demons?" It was a horrible thought.

"They must have done, or why have I got so many spells about them in my grimoire? From what I've seen so far, they certainly engaged in darker magic than we have. And you must have some demon related spells in yours."

She had to grudgingly admit she did. "I thought it was more theoretical than practical."

"Everything's theoretical until you decide to act on it."

A thought struck her. "How did you learn to do the whole lightning bolt-thing?"

"The grimoire, of course. And there's a whole lot more in there, too. No wonder someone else wants them."

They crested a rise and the hedges fell away, the headlights spilling onto the downs. Alex turned down a rutted lane and the car bounced as they raced along. Avery braced herself against the sides, hoping she wouldn't be brained on the car roof. The Alfa didn't like the uneven surface.

They could see the bleached outline of the building ahead of them, but there was no sign of El or Reuben. Alex screeched to a halt next to El's battered 4x4 Landover. They bounded out, the slamming of the car doors loud in the silence.

By unspoken agreement they looked around carefully, and the silence of the night fell around them. Nothing moved. Even the normal night sounds had fled. From here they could see White Haven, its lights twinkling, and out at sea the lights of the boats. Close by, however, there was only darkness, the downs invisible, with only a sense of the openness of the unseen landscape. Avery directed her energy so it formed a ball in her hands, ready to fling at any unwanted visitors, and then focussed her senses outwards, looking for something, anything, but there was nothing else there. Only Alex.

She looked up, but the sky above was clear, the stars unflinching, with no sign of whatever had happened earlier. Was she imagining it, or could she detect a strange smell? It was like an unnatural rot.

Satisfied there was nothing waiting to attack them, Avery walked to Alex's side, and together they headed into the remnants of the house. They passed through the shell of rooms, with their broken walls and a trace of foundation showing like bones. There was still no sign of El and Reuben.

Alex whispered, "The lines ran up the hill, remember?"

He led the way, watchful and silent. They both muffled their presence with a spell, cloaking their bodies so they appeared like shadows. The locators of El's spell were still visible, pale lines marking long vanished foundations of maybe an earlier dwelling. Within a few minutes they came to a black hole in the ground, its opening several feet below the surface. Piles of earth and stone stood either side, and a huge stone square like a flagstone lay upended to the side. The smell of rot was stronger now, coming from the hole.

"What now?" Avery asked. "If we go down there they could attack us by accident, or what if something's down there with them?" She trailed off, her meaning apparent.

"I'll look." Alex dropped to his knees and put his head in. He summoned light, and projected a pale light from his hand downwards. Avery stood close by, hoping nothing would emerge from the surrounding blackness.

After a few seconds Alex said, "It's an old cellar. Follow me."

He gripped either side of the opening and dropped from sight. As soon as he was in she took a last look around and followed him. She felt him grip her waist and hold her, gently lowering her to the ground.

A passageway snaked away from them, a pale light ahead. They had only taken a few steps when a scream rang out, and then a shout of rage. Alex ran and Avery followed, her heart pounding. She again summoned energy into a white-hot ball in her hands, and as Alex rounded a corner, he came to a stop. A few passages opened up, but only one was lit, and he again raced down it, following its turns. Another scream echoed around them; Alex stopped and she thudded into the back of him. He stepped aside quickly and for a brief second, Avery took in the room.

It was long and low, lined with rough brick and rotten timbers. The smell of rot and damp was strong. A lamp hung from the ceiling and the faint yellow light showed a wooden box on the floor against the far wall. Reuben was standing in the centre of the room facing a shadowy beast in the corner that crackled with heat. His arms and legs were wrapped in coils of flames that seemed to be trying to pull him towards the beast—or pull him apart. Reuben was straining to pull back, roaring with pain. As they entered the room, the flames disappeared, and Reuben fell to the floor.

The beast swelled in size, and red eyes glowed within its centre. Avery could just make out misshapen limbs; it exuded malevolence. It was a demon, and El struggled and writhed in its grip, screaming as flames crackled around her.

Alex ran to Reuben and dragged him back towards the entrance.

If they attacked the demon, they attacked El, but the box was intact, and it looked similar to Alex's. It must be the other grimoire. Avery directed her ball of glowing witch light at the box and shouted, "Release her, or I destroy the box."

For a second the demon waited, its flames slowed and the crackle subsided.

Avery felt rather than saw Alex move next to her. She shouted again. "I'll do it! El means more to me than the grimoire." The ball of light swelled in her hands and she stepped closer to the box. The demon needed to know she meant business. She sent the blast towards the box, engulfing it, and the demon roared with an unearthly howl.

Avery waited, the ball of light cradled within her hand again. "Release her now!"

From deep within the depths of the demon a column of fire rushed towards her and she rolled, flattening herself against the far wall as Alex threw up a shield in front of both of them. "Blast it again, Avery!"

She threw another blast at the wooden box and the demon howled again, this time flinging El to the floor as it charged across the room towards them. Avery redirected her aim to the demon and Alex joined her, battering the demon with their combined powers. Avery saw El staggering to her feet and she joined them with another blast of energy. The demon was surrounded, but it grew in size, filling the centre of the room.

The room now sizzled with heat and magic, and the white-hot blast surrounding the demon was almost blinding. Was it feeding off them? Avery was dimly aware of the dampness in the walls and the earth surrounding them, and she changed her focus, drawing on water instead. A jet of water shot from her hands and this time steam billowed around them as the demon howled with an unearthly cry that covered her skin in goose bumps. With a final flash of power the demon streamed upwards and out of the cellar, and suddenly the room was empty.

El fell to her knees and Alex rushed over to her. "Are you all right?"

"I'll be okay, I've just used a lot of energy, and that thing sucked some from me. Is Reuben all right?"

Avery felt dazed and exhausted, but she turned and checked Reuben and found him groggy and weak. "I don't know, but he's alive. We need to get out of here before that thing comes back."

"We're not going anywhere without that box," El said, standing on slightly shaky legs.

"Oh, we're definitely taking that box," Alex agreed. He looked at Avery, "Are you okay?"

She nodded. "I'm fine. I think. Better than Reuben, anyway." She turned and pulled Reuben's arm, trying to avoid the blistering already coiling around his forearms. "Hey Reuben, you need to get up. We have to get out of here."

He looked up at her, his skin ashen, his tattoos even more vivid against his pallor. Avery could see blistering around his calves, as well. He extended his hand and she pulled him to his feet.

"I feel like crap," he said with a grimace.

"We need to get Briar. She's better at healing than any of us," El said, looking worried.

"Go," Alex said. "I'll bring the box. We need to get out of here, before that thing comes back with friends."

They met at Elspeth's flat. Unlike Alex and Avery, Elspeth didn't live above her shop. She lived on the top floor of an old, converted warehouse overlooking the harbour. The walls were a mixture of warm brick and ornate dark wallpaper like her shop; the floor was made of solid oak, and the windows were long and metal framed. And it was small. "I love it, but it costs me a fortune," El had once complained. Lamplight pooled in the corners and incense filled the air—a protection spell.

They had squashed into the rickety lift and mostly fell into her flat, all of them exhausted. The wooden box was on the floor, looking ominous. Avery gazed out of the window at the harbour below, illuminated by the streetlights, and watched the gentle rise and fall of the waves and the boats bobbing gently on the swell. She could feel the box behind her. Half of her wanted to see what was in it, half of her wanted to be at home, tucked up in bed, asleep. Or maybe with Alex. She was aware of his presence everywhere, like a tickling of her senses, and she longed to touch him again.

A loud knock at the door disturbed her reverie and Briar came in, followed by Gil.

"I wasn't sure you'd be able to come," Alex told him.

Gil frowned. "Reuben's hurt. Of course I'm here." He rushed to Reuben's side. "How you doing, Reu?"

"I've been better," he said. He sat on the sofa, sipping a strong coffee. "The burns are the worst. That thing lashed me with these weird flame ropes."

"It was a demon," Alex said seriously. He stood leaning against the kitchen counter. "We have to call it what it is."

Gil and Briar looked shocked; the others were used to the term now.

"When you said it over the phone, I thought it was a joke," Briar said. She sat on the floor next to Reuben, unpacking her bottles and salves. She was pale without makeup, her hair bundled on top of her head.

"It's no joke," El murmured from where she sat in front of the fireplace, black candles burning there instead of a fire, to ward off the spirits. "That thing wrapped me up in its demon fire. I'm lucky I wasn't burnt either. I presume it needed me - maybe to open the box."

"I have some salves for burns, and a spell for spirit fire. Let's hope that helps," Briar said, choosing a pot.

"Tell us everything," Gil urged.

Alex started, telling them about the spirit walking, and then El told them about their investigations which had led to the house. She turned to Alex and Avery. "So you saw something during your spirit walk? Was it the same thing?"

"I don't know." Alex shrugged. "But we were above you and it rushed at us. It was a dark mass. It looked like the demon in the room, but it could have been someone with dark energy disguising themselves."

Avery leaned back against the window frame, its cold steel digging into her shoulder. "If the demon was controlled by necromancy, then it could be that whatever—or whoever—was spirit walking sent the demon."

Gil had been watching Briar expertly tend to Reuben's wounds, but now he looked at Avery. "You're saying somebody controlled that thing. The demon."

"Why would a demon need a spell book, Gil?" she asked. "They don't. Witches need spell books. Witches control demons. Or at least, some do. It was very popular in medieval times. And someone clearly is willing to do anything to get those grimoires."

It was a horrible thing to acknowledge, but they had to. She watched Gil and Reuben. They were both so different. Reuben the handsome surfer who had supposedly turned his back on magic, and Gil, his older, quieter brother. Gil's hair was darker and shorter, and he was slightly thicker set, but now that they sat next to each other, Avery could see the family resemblance around their eyes, and the set of their mouth.

"So instead of healing and nurturing magic, we're now dealing with dark magic?" Gil looked at Avery accusingly. "You've caused this, by finding that box and those papers."

Avery felt like she'd been punched. "Sod off, Gil! I didn't cause this! And I didn't find those papers, or even look for them. They were left to me. If you want to blame anyone, blame Anne!" She was angry now, and she could feel her magic ready to sizzle again. "In fact, blame your relative. She's the one who dragged Anne into all this."

The tension in the room was palpable as Gil stood. "We only have Anne's word for that. It could be a lie, or a double cross. Something to draw us into looking, all for someone else's purposes. Anne went to a lot of trouble to point us in the right direction. When she was dead. Very convenient."

Avery stepped towards Gil. "You had no idea about your history. Stop trying to blame someone else. It's probably your mad uncle Addison who tried to kill us tonight."

"Stop it. Both of you." Alex stepped between them and then looked at Gil. "You have to accept this, Gil, like it or not. I suggest you start looking for your own grimoire. You too, Briar. The gods only know what's in there." He turned to Avery, a ghost of a smile in his eyes. "I'll help you find yours." He then announced to all of them, "And we need to stick together. I don't know about you, but I have no idea how to summon a demon, control one, or destroy one. That thing we encountered tonight is only banished. It will be back. And we need to be ready for it."

Thirteen

A very woke late and stretched in her bed luxuriously. And then she winced. She felt as heavy as lead and she had a dull headache. Last night's activities had depleted her energy levels, and she needed to replenish them.

The sunlight filtered through her blinds and in the warm light she wondered if last night had been a nightmare. So many things had happened. The spirit walk had been magical—well, most of it. And Alex. What had happened there? The feel of his kiss still lingered on her lips, and she hoped it would happen again. And then, of course, the demon had changed everything.

She looked around at the room for reassurance; at her pictures, the shelves with her favourite objects displayed, her soft bed linen, and her old drawers and wardrobe. Here she felt safe. As she moved her feet down the bed she pushed against something heavy and heard a meow. She looked down and found Circe and Medea blinking at her. Time for breakfast.

After she'd showered, she headed down to the shop. It was only Friday, one week since she had been given the box and the letter from Anne, but it felt like a lifetime had passed.

The shop was open, and a few customers were already browsing. The mellow sounds of John Coltrane played in the background. Sally looked up as she entered. She was straightening cards and tidying shelves, but she took one look at her and said, "Let's talk."

Avery caught Dan's eyes from where he stood at the counter, and he grinned. Dan was tall, dark, and skinny, and he was far more tolerant of her erratic behaviour over the last few days than Sally.

Avery headed to the coffee pot in the back room and poured herself a large mug. She looked at Sally. "Would you like one?"

Sally leaned against the doorframe, arms folded across her chest. "Don't try to distract me, Avery. What's going on with you?" Her lips were pursed into a thin line, and she looked genuinely worried.

"Nothing's going on; I've just had a few busy days and late nights." Avery sipped her coffee and felt the warm rush of caffeine thaw her sluggish brain.

"I have never known you not come into work before—or forget to call me! And you look like shit today."

Wow, Sally wasn't pulling any punches. "Thanks, Sally. You're so sweet to notice!"

Sally sighed. "I'm saying this because I'm your friend and I'm worried about you! Your behaviour is weird."

She needed to reassure her—quickly. "The stuff I had from Anne has thrown up some questions about my family, that's all. I've just been doing some investigating. And that's meant some late nights." Sally knew her family was a touchy subject. Hopefully she wouldn't ask anything further.

"You know a woman was killed last night? I hope you haven't been wandering the streets on your own. It's not safe."

Avery almost spilled her coffee in shock. "Who was killed? Where?"

"A car was found crashed on the road over the moors. There was blood everywhere, apparently. The police aren't saying much at the moment, but there's no other cars involved, and it's really suspicious."

Avery felt dizzy and she groped for a stool. "On the moors? What—miles away?"

"No! Just outside the town." She lowered her voice. "I saw Joe this morning as I was opening up. He said he's never seen anything like it. It was like she'd been attacked by an animal."

Joe was one of the local policemen. He'd been to school with Sally and knew her well. And besides, in a small town, news travelled fast.

Avery's brain didn't seem to want to process anything. "But I thought you said it was a car accident? That can cause a lot of blood."

"Joe wouldn't say, but I think there was something else."

"So they think a crazy person did this? That there's some sort of killer in the area?"

Sally clammed up. "I don't know. But it's weird. You should be careful."

"Well, so should you, then," she retaliated. Avery desperately needed to speak to the others. *Was this a human attack, or had the demon attacked some poor woman?* As horrible as the thought was that there was a murderer on the loose, it was far preferable to a demon. "Look," she said in an effort to appease Sally, "I haven't done anything to endanger myself. Don't worry. And I'm sure this accident is just that. Okay?"

"You're heading out the door again, aren't you?"

"Just for a while. I won't be long."

Before Avery left, she went back up to her flat and covered it in every ward and protection spell she could think of, and then she protected the shop, too. She would take every precaution she could.

Avery's feet seemed to know where she was going before she did. They led her straight to the pub. Part of her wondered if it was wise to see Alex again so soon. She was confused about the kiss. *Was it something that could happen again, or was it a spur of the moment flirt that meant nothing?* Well, to him. It meant more than it should to her. As much as she might try to deny it, she was attracted to him. Maybe she should try to put up some barriers. Self-protection was a good thing.

The streets were getting busy. Shoppers meandered along the streets, enjoying the bunting that had appeared over the last few days, and shop owners were decorating their window displays for the summer Solstice. As White Haven was a town that embraced its witchy history, witch-hanging included, it also embraced the natural rhythms of the seasons, and the Solstice was one of them. Tomorrow night there'd be fires and parties on the beach, and the pubs would be offering specials. Unfortunately, at this moment, The Wayward Son was closed.

As much as she was itching to wake Alex, she figured she should let him sleep. Instead, she headed for El's shop to see how Reuben was. The door swung silently in, and she found the same woman from the other day behind the counter. Instead of letting her through, she said, "She's still at home. And I know nothing." She held her hand up to ward off further questions and Avery turned round and headed to the quay, convinced she knew more than she was letting on.

The entrance to El's flat had a big lobby with bare brick walls and a call system at the bottom. She pressed the buzzer and without needing to speak, El said, "Come on up, Avery."

Presuming the Dread Guardian of the Shop—as Avery had started to call her—had phoned ahead, Avery headed through the doors that El had released and into the lift. Within seconds she was in El's flat.

Sunlight and a light breeze streamed in through the big windows, and she saw the harbour sparkling in the sunshine, the boats bobbing on the sea. She had a moment of pleasure as she looked at the beautiful place she lived, before her eye was drawn to the box in the centre of the lounge. It was open.

El sat on the floor in front of it, objects strewn around her. She looked up at Avery. "It's similar to Alex's. A goblet, an Athame, a ritual bowl, a small chopping knife, and some jewellery—a beautiful old pendant." She held it up to the light and Avery took it from her, turning it. The silver chain was long, and the pendant was a blood red stone. She must have looked puzzled because El said, "Carnelian. To protect and confer endurance and courage. If I'm honest, it's what I need right now."

Avery dropped onto the rug next to her. "Have you heard what happened on the moor last night? After we left?"

"No. What?"

"A woman had a car accident. Except it's probably just meant to look like an accident."

El was already pale, but if it was possible, she turned paler and her hand flew to her mouth. "No!"

"Yes. I'm wondering if it was the demon."

El closed her eyes briefly. "What have we got into, Avery? This isn't what I love about magic. Demons, blood, unbridled power. I want to protect people, make them happy, tap into nature, live at one with our surroundings."

Avery snorted. "We haven't got unbridled power, and I doubt we will. Besides, we choose what we do with our magic."

"But we can't control a demon. And I'm not sure I want to."

"Good. Neither do I. But we're going to have to, because it will come for us again." Avery looked around the room and could hardly believe what she was saying on such a bright, beautiful day.

"Do we know who the woman was?"

Avery shook her head. "No. Not yet."

"Do the others know?"

Avery shrugged. "I don't know, haven't spoken to them yet." She looked around the room. "Where's Reuben?"

"Gil took him home; he wanted to keep an eye on him." El's pretty face fell into a sullen frown. "I don't think he trusted me."

"He's his younger brother—he's just worried."

"The thing is, Reuben didn't even argue. I think he's mad at me. He barely looked at me as he left."

Avery wasn't sure before, but she was sure now. El and Reuben definitely had something between them. El looked like she might cry. Avery patted her shoulder. "He had a horrible shock. He knows you, and he knows what you are. Hell, he's a witch, too! He'll come round. He might even accept his gifts." Avery nodded towards the box. "What about the grimoire? The box is virtually identical to Alex's. Different markings, but that's all. The grimoire must be in the lid."

El seemed pleased to focus on something else. "They're runes again. One to protect against spirits and demons, but the ones around the lid are different. I'm not opening it here, though. Not alone. I was thinking of bringing it to our Solstice celebration tomorrow. I want to open it while we're all together."

"Okay," Avery nodded. "Seems sensible." Although under the potency of a waning gibbous moon, and in the open, they might attract more than they were ready for. However, she kept her thoughts to herself. "We're celebrating in my small garden. It's already warded and protected, and I'll add to that today."

They both jumped as the intercom rang loudly. El headed over and pushed the button. "Hi, Elspeth here."

"This is Detective Inspector Newton. We'd like to ask you a few questions, please."

El looked at Avery in shock, and mouthed Shit! She turned quickly to the intercom. "Certainly, can I ask what about?"

"We'll explain when we see you." He sounded stern, and Avery felt her stomach flip. "Are you going to let us in?"

"Of course, come on up." She pressed the release button and turned to Avery, stricken. "Bollocks, and triple bollocks!" And then her gaze fell on the box, which even in the bright sunlight looked distinctly magical.

"We'll cover it with a spell," Avery said quickly. "Help me drag it to the corner."

El ran over and between them they wrestled it under a table as Avery quickly murmured a spell that made the box invisible.

"What can they want, Avery?"

"Maybe they saw your car on a camera. Stay calm. You were going for a drive in the moonlight and saw nothing. That's allowed, you know."

They were interrupted by a knock at the door, and after a final look around the room, El went to the door, while Avery stood in the kitchen making tea and trying to calm her nerves.

El opened the door and without waiting for an invitation, a tall man with dark hair swept into the room, followed by a younger man with reddish hair. They both looked around, stopping briefly when they saw Avery, and then finally looked at El. She now looked very composed and shaking their hands said, "Hi, I'm Elspeth. Please come in." She gestured further into the room.

The dark haired man spoke first. "Detective Inspector Newton, and this is Officer Moore."

Moore nodded and followed the DI into the room. They seemed to fill the space of El's small flat. Avery thought Newton looked as if he was in his mid-thirties, and he was handsome, the clean lines of his face exuding both confidence and suspicion. He wore a single-breasted grey suit and a crisp white shirt, and it looked good on him. Moore's suit, in comparison, looked a little rumpled.

Avery came out from behind the open-plan kitchen counter and shook their hands as well, trying very hard to make a good impression. "Hi, I'm Avery, El's friend."

Newton nodded, looking her up and down. "I know your face. You run the occult store."

"The bookstore," she corrected him, a stone in her stomach. All storeowners had regular interactions with the police as part of community policing and safety, however she had never met Newton before. "Can I get you some tea? I'm making some anyway."

"No thanks." His face was grim, and he turned to El. "There was a death last night on the road across the moors. We've been combing the footage of the cameras leading out of town along that road, and your car was seen leaving at 11:07 PM and coming back into town around 1:15 AM. Where had you been?"

"Just out for a drive. I like to sit on the cliff top and look over the sea. I also found out recently that my old family home used to be the old Hawk House, up on the moor. I wanted to see it."

"At night?" he asked, watching El closely, every now and again flicking a glance at Avery, while Moore scribbled away.

Avery risked a glance under the far table, and satisfied that the box couldn't be seen, busied herself with tea.

"I was with Reuben. It seemed romantic, you know, gazing at the stars." She smiled and winked, but Newton ignored her.

"Who's Reuben?"

"Reuben Jackson. He's a local. Works at Greenlane Nursery."

"One of the Jacksons from Greenlane Manor?" he asked, his eyes narrowing.

El nodded, "Yes."

He glanced at Moore, who again scribbled furiously, and then asked, "Did you see anything on the moors?"

"Nothing, except a few passing cars. Why?"

"You didn't hear anything?"

El folded her arms across her chest. "No. Why are you asking me questions if there was a car accident? I mean, I'm sorry that someone is dead, but I didn't see anything. I would have stopped, obviously. And I certainly didn't hit anyone, you can check my car."

Newton hesitated a moment and glanced again at Moore, who gave the faintest of nods. He looked at El and then beyond her to where Avery stood, now sipping tea and desperately trying to calm her rapidly beating heart. "We're not worried about another car. We're worried about something far darker."

He watched them and the silence in the room seemed to solidify, anchoring Avery to the spot. "What do you mean, 'darker?'" El asked.

He changed tack. "You two, and a few others in White Haven, have a certain reputation."

"We do?" Elspeth said, looking confused.

He smiled, unpleasantly. "Yes. And while some people may think it's interesting, even exciting, I think it's dangerous."

"Detective Inspector, you're going to have to be a bit clearer with that. I really don't know what you mean," El said, remaining very composed. Maybe there was a flicker of glamour there, too. Avery silently applauded her.

"Magic, is what I mean," he said looking her straight in the eye. "Magic that uses the laws of nature for her own ends."

Avery's eyebrows shot up, but El continued smoothly. "Magic respects nature, it does not abuse it, and neither do I. While I may have a certain reputation, it's all for the good. I sell simple trinkets, necklaces, bracelets, and rings that have the natural properties of the gemstones I use. That's not magic."

"So why do people whisper that if they need certain charms or protections, they should visit your shop?"

"I merely capitalise on the glamour of magic, but I'm just a silversmith."

He looked across the room to where Avery stood silently watching and feeling quite annoyed. "And you. You sell books on the occult, mysticism, divination, tarot cards."

"I also sell books of romance, action, thrillers, and fantasy. It's not illegal," she said, her anger building. "This is not the dark ages. This town has a rich history, built on the witch-hunts and the burning. If you haven't noticed, the whole town is full of soothsayers, fortune tellers, herbalists, and angel believers. That's why tourists come here. I sell what people are interested in." She could feel a breeze whipping up around her again, and she saw Newton narrow his eyes as a strand of hair lifted in front of her face. She quickly tucked it behind her ear.

His grey eyes darkened like a storm. "The woman on the road had had her throat ripped out. Car accidents don't do that."

El's hand flew to her chest and Avery gasped and said, "I'm sorry to hear that, truly sorry, but we had nothing to do with it." She hesitated a second, and then thought she should come clean—after all, he'd have seen Alex's car. "I was with Alex Bonneville last night; I know you'll have seen his car, too. We met El at Hawk House, but that's all. We didn't see anything, either."

Newton's face was like granite. "So you all met at the Hawk House site, a couple of days before the Solstice, and a young woman died violently."

"I can assure you, those events are not connected," Avery said, her voice icy as she glared back at Newton.

"We'll need to speak to Alex Bonneville and Reuben Jackson." Newton gave them both a long, searching look, and then he looked around the room carefully, as if something would suddenly reveal itself. "That's all for now. Do *not* repeat what we told you about the way the woman died. If you think of anything, come and see me. And don't go anywhere."

He pulled his card out and laid it on the coffee table, while Moore pocketed his notebook. He had said nothing throughout the entire interview, and he followed Newton silently out the door.

As soon as they had left, Avery snorted. "Don't go anywhere! Where the hell does he think we'd go? I live here!"

"Holy shit, Avery. We're persons of interest in a murder investigation and a woman is dead!" El collapsed on the sofa and Avery walked over and sat next to her, cradling her now lukewarm tea and bringing one for El. They were silent for a few moments, and Avery leaned back, closing her eyes, trying to rationally think through the events of the night.

El interrupted her thoughts. "What do we know about demons, Avery?"

"Not much. Dark entities that need blood or souls to feed on—powerful, unruly, vengeful, and they don't belong in our world. They can be summoned and controlled with necromancy. If you're insane." She opened her eyes to find El staring at her. "Well, that's what I know. What about you?"

"The same. To be honest, I never thought they were real. I thought they were a magical figment that belonged in the dark ages. Manifestations of people's fear."

"Well, it wasn't a manifestation last night. It killed someone and attacked Reuben."

"If it's here, it will kill again. We have to stop it."

"So now we have three problems," Avery said. "We have a premonition, a suspicious detective, and whoever's attacking us and their pet demon to sort out. I better let Alex know he's going to get visitors, and you need to tell Reuben." And then she pulled her phone from her bag.

Avery decided she wanted the rest of her day to be normal, without any more drama. She stopped at the bakery and brought a selection of cakes, pastries, and three double-shot lattes with a sprinkling of cinnamon. When she arrived at the shop at just after eleven, she found Dan sitting on a stool behind the counter, reading a book. The music had changed, and Led Zeppelin's "Kashmir" was now playing.

"Hi," she grinned, trying to put her nerves behind her. "I've bought snacks."

There were only a couple of customers in the shop, browsing in the thriller section, so she plonked the goods down on the shop counter and took a long drink of coffee. Sometimes she felt caffeine was the only thing getting her through the day.

"So the wanderer returns!" Dan said with a wry smile, and he put his book down and reached for a latte. "This is great. Cheers."

"Quiet morning?" Avery asked.

"A bit of a rush earlier, but it's quietened down now. What have you been up to? You've made Sally a very grumpy woman."

Avery decided to come clean. "I've been questioned by the police, actually. All because me and Alex took a late night drive out to the moors."

Dan's face fell. "That poor woman. But they questioned you? I thought it was an accident?"

"A suspicious accident," Avery explained, not wanting to say more. "Anyway, I think he was happy-ish with our explanation. Obviously, we know nothing." Which wasn't strictly true, but she wasn't about to go talking about demons. Dan would think she was mad. In fact, she might be. "Where is Sally?" she asked, looking around.

"Out the back. Sally!" he yelled. "Coffee's here." He reached for a pastry. "Wow, these are awesome."

"Oh, you're back!" Sally said, coming from the back room, a mixture of relief and annoyance on her face. She looked at the coffee and cakes. "A peace offering?"

"Sort of. Sorry, Sally. It's been a hell of a week."

Dan spoke through a mouthful of pastry, "And she's been interviewed by the police."

"But I'm fine," Avery rushed to calm Sally. "It's just a misunderstanding."

Sally leaned closer, glancing at the customers to make sure they were out of hearing range, and said quietly, "Things have changed since you picked up Anne's stuff. Why?"

"It's nothing," Avery said, also leaning forward. "She just gave me some family histories, that's all."

"We both know about your—" she hesitated for a second, "practices. And it's the Solstice. Do you need our help?"

Avery was so shocked that she almost spit her coffee out. "What do you mean—'practices?'"

Dan smiled. "This is a witchy town, but we all know there's more witch in some of us than others. And that includes *you*, Avery. And don't panic."

"I make no secret of my interests," she started, defensively.

"Oh bollocks, Avery. We're not talking interests. We're talking practices," Dan said, brushing pastry flakes from his shirt. "We respect your abilities, but they're not a secret, not to us, anyway."

Avery felt the hairs stand up on the back of her neck. She had tried so hard to hide her powers, and she hoped they didn't know the scope of them. She must have looked shocked because Sally added, "Don't worry; only a few people really know. Locals. We respect your privacy. But if something weird is going on, they will start to ask questions. We know you're *safe*, but magic is magic, Avery."

They both fell silent as Avery sipped her coffee and tried to think of something to say. Today was going to be one of those days, and with the impending Solstice, it could be weirder than most. "All right," she said, making her mind up and glancing once more over her shoulder. "I have certain abilities. It's hereditary. I am safe with my abilities, as in, *I do not intend harm*, but there are others who do. Things may not be so safe around here at the moment, so I want you both to be careful. I'll prepare something for you to carry, and I want you to promise me to carry it always. At least for a while."

Dan and Sally's slightly jokey tone now disappeared. "So something is going on?" Sally asked.

"Yes. But that's all I'm saying. Now, if you don't mind, I'm going to head upstairs and prepare a little something for you." She looked at their shocked faces and allowed herself a small laugh. "Well, you did ask."

Avery headed up to her flat and first checked her main living area to ensure nothing remotely magical lay around, just in case DI Newton wanted to visit, and then she did the same in the attic. She shoved the wooden box into the working area, where her shelves were filled with her supplies, and performed a spell to dissuade visitors from looking too hard in that particular area.

Satisfied with her work, she crossed the small back alley to the walled garden and entered it through the ornately decorated gate that was imbued with spells. She always kept it locked, but it also had protection added to it to ward off prying eyes. Once inside, she looked around with pleasure and sighed in relief. Her garden always calmed her.

It was surrounded with four high walls covered with climbers and espaliered fruit trees. It seemed bigger than it really was, because it was impossible to see it all from one spot. Pergolas and gazebos added height and structure, and everywhere you looked the plants were growing with a giddy profusion. There were roses, irises, dahlias, verbenas, geraniums, lavender, hollyhocks, delphiniums, lupins, shrubs and small trees, and much more. Gravel paths wound through everything, and everywhere she walked, she brushed by plants so that their perfume filled the air.

She bypassed the garden table and chairs where she had seen Alex the other night, and pressed on to where the herbs grew. She stopped and filled a basket with a variety of cuttings, and decided she'd come back later as the light fell to collect some roots. They were best gathered at dusk.

They would welcome the Solstice here tomorrow, and they would be undisturbed. In the centre of the garden was a grassed area, as smooth as velvet and perfect for rituals. Although the garden was surrounded by other buildings, only her own flat was high and close enough to see into it.

Avery saw Dan and Sally once more before the end of the day to give them their hex bags. She called them into the back room, and left the door part way open to watch for customers. "Here you go," she said.

Dan looked bemused at the small muslin bag that was filled with herbs and tied at the neck with cord. "What do I do with it?"

"Wear it." She pulled the cord free of the bag. "See, you can hang it around your neck, tucked under your shirt, or put it in your pocket. Whatever you choose. Just wear it."

Sally looked at her wide-eyed. "It just looks like the herbs I put in my underwear drawer. Does it *do* anything?"

"It does plenty. Just take it and use it," Avery said.

Sally leaned forward and touched it gingerly, and then lifted it over her head like a necklace so it rested under her shirt, as Avery had suggested, while Dan put his in his jeans' pocket.

Avery felt as if a huge weight had been lifted off her shoulders, and although she was sure that feeling wouldn't last long, she decided to enjoy it while it lasted. It was nice to be able to be even a little bit honest with two people who weren't witches. "Excellent, now, be careful."

"What are you doing for the rest of the day?" Dan asked. "We're going to The Mermaid for a pint if you want to come?"

Avery shook her head. "No, I'm having a quiet night, thanks. Just me, the cats, and the TV."

"You sure?" Sally said, looking worried.

"Absolutely. See you in the morning."

Once they'd gone and the shop was locked up, Avery enjoyed the laziest night she could, not even wanting to look at Anne's research. The previous night's events had exhausted her, and the woman's death had depressed her. Magic was the last thing she wanted to do. And besides, the Solstice would be a busy day.

Fourteen

Saturdays were always busy, customers streaming in and out of the shop, and all the talk was about the celebrations on the beach later. Avery, like many others, had decorated her shop window. The day passed in a whirl of chat and sales, and she barely had time to think about their own celebrations that night.

Neither Dan nor Sally made any mention of their conversation from the previous day, and Avery was relieved. On his way out the door, Dan asked, "Are you going to any of the celebrations on the beach later?"

"No. I'll be celebrating privately tonight. Are you?"

He grinned. "Sure, who doesn't enjoy a good bonfire, a bit of chanting by our local pagan druid, and a few beers?"

She laughed. One of the town councillors liked to officiate at the solstice and equinox celebrations, proclaiming himself the local druid. Visitors and locals loved it, although there was no real magic involved at all. The crowds should be enough to keep the demon and whoever was controlling it away. "Good. Stay with the crowds. And enjoy!"

The pale blue sky seemed like a lid on the town, trapping the heat of the day within the lanes and buildings. One of the pleasures of mid-summer, Avery thought, was the light that lasted late into the night. She headed into the garden, spending the next few hours preparing for the other witches' arrival, and trying to ignore her growing hunger pangs. Some magic needed an empty stomach so Avery hadn't eaten since breakfast.

They had decided to celebrate the solstice with a very non-witchy BBQ after their celebration. Avery's brick-built BBQ hadn't been used since the previous summer, so she scrubbed it clean. She prepared salads for later, and made sure there were plenty of candles to supplement the low electric lighting that illuminated the garden paths, plants, and the table; the whole place would look pretty and magical.

Alex arrived first, letting himself through the gate. Avery heard the crunch of the gravel as he headed down the path. She sat at the table sipping water and smiled as he came into view. Last week, she had wanted to strangle him, but now her heart raced a little quicker as she remembered that long, lingering kiss.

He sank into the chair opposite hers. "How you doing?"

"I've been better."

He placed his proffered beer in the cooler and took a swig of water. "Thanks for the heads-up yesterday. DI Newton arrived with his silent witness in tow. What a creepy pair they are."

"They *do* have a murder to investigate."

"I know. I'm trying to make light of a bad situation. I'm not normally suspected of murder." He looked around. "I can feel you've increased your protection."

"Yep. And I gave Dan and Sally an amulet bag, too."

He raised his eyebrows.

"Apparently, a few locals know I'm a witch—and you too, probably. They mentioned *others* and I didn't ask. I'm really not sure how much they know of what we actually can do, but we're trusted to do the right thing, apparently. So I did. Has anyone ever said anything to you?"

"About magic? Never. But I work in a pub, not an occult bookstore. And I think people associate women far more with witches than men. Doesn't sound like they'll be hounding you out of town, anyway," Alex said with a grin. "Did you ask El what happened at Hawk House—you know, how the demon arrived?"

"No, Newton arrived before I'd had a chance to find out. We'll ask later."

His eyes darkened and his gaze fell to her lips, and it seemed he was going to say something when the gate opened again, and she heard El and Briar arrive. Avery wasn't sure if she was relieved or disappointed.

Briar was looking her most ethereal. Her dark hair was loose and she wore white everything—a long skirt and a lace-trimmed cotton shirt. El was wearing her usual black, and her white-blonde hair glowed in the evening light. She was carrying a large object wrapped in a blanket.

"No Gil yet?" El asked.

"No. Any news from Reuben?" Avery asked.

"No," El answered, with a slight grimace.

Briar looked at all of them. "I feel I'm missing something."

"We'll hang on for Gil and then we'll fill you in," Avery said. "What are you carrying, El?"

"I've brought a sword, bound with ceremonial magic. I thought it would be great to draw our circle." She unwrapped it and Avery's jaw dropped in amazement.

"Wow! That's so cool!"

The sword had a simple hilt, a mix of silver and what looked like copper. The blade had a fine engraving running down the centre. Alex leapt to his feet. "May I?"

El grinned. "Of course."

Alex lifted it and then swished it around. "I like this."

"Better not let Newton see you with it, or he'll be accusing you all over again," Avery said.

Briar was silent, but she watched Alex admiringly, and for a second Avery felt a flash of guilt as she remembered their kiss from last night. She was sure Briar fancied him, but it seemed Alex was oblivious. His muscles flexed as he moved, and Avery felt desire stir within her.

El laughed. "Seriously, Alex, you're holding it all wrong." She stepped in to adjust his grip when Gil arrived, surprising everyone when Reuben appeared behind him.

For a second El didn't move, she just looked at Reuben with wide, questioning eyes, and the place fell silent for a brief second as Alex strode towards them. "Gil, good to see you. Reu, how are you? We've been worried sick."

Despite the attack a couple of nights before, Reuben looked as handsome and rugged as ever, and he broke into a grin. "It'll take more than a demon to finish me off." He looked serious for a moment. "Thanks for your help the other night. Without you two," he glanced at Avery, "things would have been very different." He looked at El. "How are you?"

Relief washed over her face. She had been so worried he wouldn't forgive her. "Feeling guilty. I could have killed you."

"No, the demon could have. It wasn't your fault. You could have died, too."

"What about the burns?"

Reuben showed the angry red welts at his wrists, arms, and legs. "They're still there, but they're healing—thanks to Briar's poultice."

Avery relaxed, relieved that El and Reuben seemed to be okay.

Gil sat at the table. "Well, I'm pissed at all of you. This is still insanity to me."

Alex put the sword on the table. "You'd better get used to it, because it's not going away."

Gil looked up at him. "I don't appreciate the police coming to visit, either."

"Neither do I!"

"Or me!" El added, annoyed.

Briar intervened. "The police? What's happened since I last saw you?"

"Didn't you hear?" Avery asked, having a feeling she was about to ruin Briar's night. "A woman died on the moors that night."

She nodded. "A car accident. What's that got to do with us?"

"It wasn't a car accident. It was the demon."

Briar looked horrified as the reality of their situation sank in. "The one that attacked you?"

"Well, there better not be another," Alex said dryly. He turned to El. "How did it attack you? You never said."

"We were already underground," she said, thinking. "The spell showed us the foundation and led us to the underground cellar's entrance. Up to that point we were alone. Obviously it was dark, but I didn't sense anything, and there wasn't a sound, except for the occasional car on the road beyond. It arrived once we were in the cellar room with the box. I don't know where it came from—it was just there. I didn't sense a thing." She exhaled heavily. "I feel pretty stupid. It grabbed me and it was like being held by a cord of electricity. It was horrible. I could sense this darkness and hunger for power. And I couldn't get free—that was really scary."

Reuben stirred. "It's true. It was just there. As it grabbed El, it struck me."

"But the box was there," Avery said, puzzled. "Why didn't it take it?"

"The wards," Briar said. "They would have repelled it."

Alex nodded. "Good point. Maybe the demon was to keep you there until whoever was controlling it could get there to get the box. We're lucky we were closer."

Gil stood up. "If I'm honest, I'm not feeling that celebratory. However, we are here to celebrate the Solstice, so let's get on with it."

"Well, I'm going to celebrate my first encounter with a demon and surviving," Reuben said with a grin.

"Good point!" Alex agreed. "So, you're joining us?"

"After last night, I've decided I can't ignore my magic any longer. Especially if I want to survive. So yes, I am."

"Before we start, I need a hand to get the box in," El said. "You're all going to help me get my grimoire."

They stood on the grassed area in the centre of the garden. El held the sword with the point turned down, touching the earth, and starting in the East, she walked around in a full circle, large enough to hold all of them. The other five followed, all murmuring the ritual words to create the circle.

They stepped into it, and as the circle was sealed behind them, Avery felt the outside world falling away as the sacred space enveloped her. All other evening sounds disappeared: cars, the murmur of people talking that carried from the road, and even the sound of the breeze rustling through the trees.

They had decided their celebrations should encompass giving thanks to the gods and the elements for their magic and an appeal to give strength for the coming year. They spoke in unison, their voices weaving together as they repeated the well-known lines, rising and falling with changing cadence. They moved around the sacred space in a steady dance, exchanging candles between them, and Avery acutely felt the cold grass beneath her feet, dry and brittle.

As the light diminished and the first stars appeared in the sky, Avery felt the turn in the season, the acknowledgement that they were moving towards winter already, the longest day almost over. With the silence came power, and she felt it soaking into her skin and bones, renewing her for the challenges she knew were to come. Within the circle, the candlelight at the four points of the compass burned steadily, throwing a flickering light over their ritual, but outside it was black, and it seemed to press in on them.

Avery had no idea how long the ritual lasted. Time within the circle seemed to slow, but her gaze fell on the box in the centre, and she wondered if opening it would be as challenging to El as Alex's was to him.

Gil broke the silence that had fallen at the end of the ritual. "When do you want to open your box, El?"

"Now's as good a time as any." She walked over to the box, opening the lid, which like Alex's was deep with small runes carved around the edge.

"Are all the grimoires hidden in boxes?" Briar asked, watching El carefully.

"Maybe," Avery said. Briar looked worried, and Avery still wasn't sure if she wanted to find hers at all.

Reuben spoke from opposite Avery, his face in the shadows. "It's interesting, isn't it? If we find another one like this, we have to presume they were all hidden together."

"It makes sense though, doesn't it?" Gil said. "The Witchfinder was on his way, and they all needed to hide their grimoires. Perhaps they'd had the boxes prepared for some time."

"How do you want to play this, El?" Alex asked. He stood next to Avery, and his strong presence resonated beside her. As if he sensed her looking, he glanced at her and winked, and she felt her stomach flip. Now was not the time to think about their kiss, and she looked back to El.

El sighed. "I have no idea. I'll say the runes as you did, Alex, and hope for the best. I've written them all down. Are you ready for whatever may emerge?"

"As ready as I'll ever be." Gil looked at Reuben. "Are you sure you want to be in the circle?"

"I'll be fine, brother."

"Is blood needed again?" Gil asked, disapproval in his voice.

"No." El sat cross-legged in front of the box, took a deep breath, and started the incantation.

Much as when Alex had started reading his runes, Avery felt the air pressure change, becoming heavy, as if it was smothering her. El's voice filled the air, and for several seconds, nothing happened. The pressure continued to build and then shapes began to manifest around them. Avery blinked, thinking she was seeing things, before they became clear. Large, black crows screeched and flapped their wings, buffeting the air. In seconds, there seemed to be hundreds of them. She shouted and pushed a crow away as it flew at her face, scratching and clawing, and then more flew at her, tangling in her hair. She could barely see; the circle was full of them and they had nowhere to go. She was dimly aware of Alex and Gil on either side, also struggling against the onslaught.

They had to open the circle.

As Avery struggled to the East to open the doorway, she fell to her knees and grabbed the sword. She uttered spells of banishment, but nothing worked. If anything, the crows were multiplying. She could hear shrieks and swearing, and she tried to protect her eyes as she rose once more to her feet. El remained seated in a private bubble of protected space, the crows unable to touch her. An enormous *crack* resounded, and she glimpsed the lid flying open, split in half.

In three swift movements Avery drew the sides of the door and opened the circle, breaking the wall of protection. The air pressure dropped like a stone, and the crows streamed past her. She fell to her knees once more and covered her head with her arms until she felt the rush of beating wings subside. Then she heard the *boom* of her protective spells breaking, and looking up, saw the arrival of large, dark shadows in the garden beyond their circle.

Demons.

Alex yelled, "Avery!" He pulled her behind him and taking the sword, quickly closed the circle again before the demons could step inside.

All six witches quickly faced outwards, bracing themselves for attack. El was seemingly unharmed after the spell.

Two demons prowled around them. Like at Hawk House, their forms were hulking black shadows with misshapen limbs, but their red eyes glowed.

Briar's voice shook. "I know you told me what happened the other night, but I didn't really picture it. I still can't believe it."

"My injuries not enough for you, Briar?" Reuben said snarkily.

"Hey, look on the bright side," Alex said. "Whoever it is, sent two. We must be a bigger threat than they thought."

Gil sounded as shocked as Briar. "What are we going to do now?"

The demons moved closer to the protective wall around them, as if testing it for weak spots. As they touched the wall, a bright blue flash crackled like electricity. The demon roared and released a stream of flame at the wall and it lit up again, shielding them. Avery knew that no matter how good their protection was, it would give way eventually.

"El, maybe you should check that book to see if there is anything on demon banishment," Alex suggested. "Reuben, you okay?"

"I'd like some revenge." Reuben clenched his hands into fists.

"I'm not sure punching them will work. Will your magic be strong enough?"

"Combined with everyone else's, yes."

"How did you banish them last time?" Gil asked, his eyes never leaving the prowling demons.

"Fire seemed to strengthen it, but it didn't like water. I pulled the water from the walls, combined it with energy, and blasted it. It just disappeared," Avery said, thinking about the chaotic fight.

"Well, there's six of us, and two of them, so I figure we have good odds," Alex said. "But, we need a plan. Renewing the protective spell will only trap us here all night. Have you got a pond in your garden, Avery?"

"Not really—it's a tiny, ornamental thing," she said thinking of the small pond by her herb garden.

While they talked, the demons prowled, pulsing with power, their shadowy mass growing and shrinking as if they were breathing. They had split up and were attacking them from opposite sides, enveloping them in flames. The walls around them again crackled with a blue, protective light.

"We're going to have to break the protection spell to attack," Gil said.

"Not until we have a plan!" Alex said, his voice curt.

While Gil and Alex argued about what to use to banish the demons, El crouched on the floor, flicking through the grimoire, desperate for something they could use. She looked at Avery, frustrated. "I can barely read a word of this, especially in this light."

Briar interrupted. "There's water in the earth, Avery, lots of it. We just need to draw it out."

"And add wind, lots of wind," Reuben suggested. "This is not their environment. If we add enough elements, it will surely overwhelm them."

Alex looked excited. "It's worth a shot. Gil—you, Briar, and Reuben draw on water and earth together, and we'll support Avery with wind."

"I have another suggestion," El said. "Use the sword to channel the elements. Either air or water. It will act as a conduit."

"Brilliant idea," Alex agreed. "I think air will work better, though, if that's okay with you, Briar?"

"No problem."

They all nodded in agreement, and Avery saw El put the grimoire back in the box and cover it as best she could. Alex gave Avery the sword. "Let's dissolve the circle together."

They stood back-to-back, hands held, saying the words that ended their protection. Within seconds the demons rushed at them, shooting long, forked tongues of flames that flickered like whips around them. Avery felt the white-hot lash of one as it whipped across her bare arms and she suppressed the urge to scream. She focussed only on air and the cold metal of the sword. Fortunately, her anger was enough to draw it quickly—it was the element that leapt quickest to her aid, as if it was always waiting to be called on. Instinctively, Alex and El had broken off from the others and now all three stood together, surrounded by a whipping vortex of wind. As one, they directed it at the demons, while the other three sent a deluge of water at the same time.

A tornado of wind, rain, and damp earth surrounded them all, blinding in its intensity, and Avery heard a shriek. She couldn't be sure if it came from the demons or one of them. The demons continued to lash out with tongues of fire, but struggled against the onslaught of elements.

Avery gathered their combined power and focussed it into one massive blast. The sword felt like an extension of her being, and her power seemed to magnify down it and beyond, directing it like a laser. She wielded it quickly, slashing back and forth as the air howled and her hair whipped around her. The group's combined attack was too strong, and soon the demons disappeared.

As Avery lowered her energy, the wind dropped. She thought she'd feel exhausted, but adrenalin soared through her. Her fingers tingled and her awareness was razor sharp.

She looked around at the others standing in a ragged line. Although the wind, rain, and earth had just raged around them, they all stood untouched. She grinned. "We did it!" Every single one of them looked at her in shock. "What's the matter?"

Alex pointed at the ground. "Feel anything different, Avery?"

She looked down and found she was hovering about a foot above the earth. Avery wasn't sure if she felt panic-stricken or excited. No, she was definitely excited. She looked up at them again. "How am I doing this? Oh, wow! This is so cool!"

"Can you stop it?" El asked, bemused. She paced around Avery, as if she was looking for strings.

She giggled. "I'm not sure I want to!"

"It might cause a problem with the locals, though," Alex observed, also trying not to laugh.

Avery heard a cry from Briar and saw her look at her feet. Although less obvious than Avery's response to the wind element, Briar's feet were now buried up to her ankles in soil. "You too, Briar," she said.

"It must be as if the elements recognise us," Briar said, as she pulled her feet out with a grimace. And then a smile flashed across her face. "You know, I was so busy with that demon that I didn't think, but it was an incredibly grounding and powerful experience. For a few seconds, I felt I could do that all night."

Gil didn't look amused at all. "Fun though this is, those demons might come back, and I'm not sure I have enough juice to do that again. I'm not sure that your garden will survive, either. It's a bit worrying that your protection spells didn't last, Avery." He lit the candles again with a turn of his wrist and all the garden lighting flickered on, too, illuminating the darkness beyond.

Avery saw chaos beyond their circle. Plants had been lifted and flung out of position, and her lawn was churned up, as if a herd of elephants had trampled across it. As reality hit her, her energy levelled out and she slowly floated back to the grass, her feet gently touching the ground.

"El, your book!" she cried with alarm, suddenly remembering the grimoire.

El turned and headed to the box, lifting the lid carefully, but she sighed with relief. "It's fine. It was protected enough, especially in the middle of all of us."

Briar was kneeling down, her hand on the earth. "I can help put your garden back together, Avery. You just need to leave me to it."

"Well, I'm starved," Alex said, running his hand through his hair and scratching his head. "I'll get the BBQ going while someone helps Avery renew our protection. Nothing ruins a good BBQ like demons."

By the time Avery returned to the BBQ area with Gil, the smells of sausages, burgers, chicken, and onions was wafting around them. She was starving. Battling demons was a good way to work up an appetite.

Strings of fairy lights were draped in the trees and they twinkled like fire flies, and candles illuminated the table. The smell of incense and sage mixed with the smell of grilled food. Someone had performed a cleansing ritual, purging the space of any negativity left by the demons.

Alex was wearing an apron and sipping beer while turning sausages on the grill. He threw her a grin as she joined them. Reuben was sitting next to El, beer in hand, looking through the grimoire. Whatever had driven him away from magic seemed to have gone, and he appeared to be as interested in the book as all of them.

Avery pulled a few beers from the chilly bin of water, and giving Gil one, chinked his and took a long drink as she sat down at the table.

Reuben looked up. "Where's Briar?"

"Still healing my garden," Avery said. "Oh no, here she is."

Briar walked into the light like a garden spirit, except the bottom of her white dress and her feet were muddy. "I think I need a shower," she said, and she tried to brush the dirt from her hands. "The good news is, your garden will survive, but I suggest you turn the hose on it tomorrow."

"Thanks, Briar," Avery grinned. She handed her a beer. "Grab a seat."

"So, what delights are in that book?" Gil asked, with a weary tone. He dropped into the seat next to Reuben.

Reuben looked baffled. "Weird stuff. Diagrams, spells, and what looks like alchemy."

"It's definitely alchemy," Elspeth said. She leaned back in her chair. "I have simpler versions in my usual grimoire, but these spells have much more detail. There are spells here to trap powers into metal, and protection spells that are sealed in rings or lockets. There's also a spell that traps a person's essence into a sealed jar."

"Essence! What's a person's essence?" Avery asked, alarmed.

"Their soul."

Silence fell, broken only by Alex dropping his metal spatula. "Is that a joke?" he asked, leaving the grill and coming over to the table.

El looked very serious. "No. And don't even ask me to read the spell out. It's hideous. And no, I won't ever try it."

Avery felt sick imagining murder, torture, and worse. "Do you think anyone has tried it?"

"Well, it's in there, isn't it?" Gil pointed out. He stood up, his chair scraping back loudly against the gravel. He paced around the table. "I told you I didn't like this. We don't do this kind of magic."

"And we're not going to," Alex said, looking in annoyed amazement at Gil. "We're not bloody animals. I've got a knife, but I'm not about to start stabbing someone!"

Avery laughed. "He's right, Gil. There are thousands of things we could do every day, but we don't. We still exercise our judgement."

"I suppose so," Gil said. "I guess I'm worried what I'll find in my book. It makes me think our ancestors were crazy."

Reuben shook his head and frowned. "I don't think they were. They were people, like us—just a bit closer to their magical roots."

"Well, considering what's happened over the past few days, I've decided I will look for mine," Briar said. She had a streak of dirt across her cheek, and as she brushed her hair back from her face, she added another one. "We can't run away from our past, especially since it seems to be insistently knocking on our door."

"Do you know where to look?" Gil asked, finally sitting again.

"Not yet. Do you?"

"Well, it seems our mad great-uncle hunted everywhere for it, so I'm wondering if it's on our grounds at all. What about you, Avery?"

"I know where my old ancestor used to live. It doesn't mean it's still there, though. And besides, someone else is living there now."

El had returned to looking at her grimoire, but now she stirred. "You know where Helena lived?"

"Yes. Well, I think so. I presume it's where she lived."

"Have you ever been to the witch museum?"

"Er, no. Well, not since I was a child," Avery said, wondering where El was going with this. "I feel self-conscious there. Why?"

El looked thoughtful. "There's something about Helena there—I visited the place when I first moved here. We should go tomorrow."

"Yes, I'm sure there'll be instructions for the hidden grimoire on display," Gil said with a note of impatience.

"Actually, it has a detailed history of the Witchfinder's visit. There may be more there than we realise, now that we're looking at it with fresh eyes."

"Awesome. I've got plenty of staff on tomorrow so I can get out for a few hours." Alex said, interrupting them. "Food's up. And while we eat, we can discuss our witches' day out." He grinned at Avery and she felt her stomach flip *again*. He really was too damn sexy for his own good.

Fifteen

In the end only El, Briar, Alex and Avery met at the museum. Reuben had persuaded Gil that it was time to search their grounds for the grimoire, and reluctantly, Gil had agreed.

The museum was a solidly constructed stone-walled, low-roofed, sixteenth century building that looked like a pub. It was close to the quay and had a small car park next to it. They had agreed to get there early so it would be quiet, but had a shock at the entrance to find a police car and yellow tape across the front door.

"Oh no, what now?" Briar said, worry creasing her face.

Avery felt fear pricking its way up her spine. "It could just be a break in?"

"Let's hope so. I think we should get out of here," Alex said, and he started to walk away, pulling Avery and El with him.

Unfortunately, before they could go anywhere, a dark sedan pulled up and DI Newton stepped out, the silent Moore exiting the other door.

"What a surprise to see you here," Newton said, his tone accusatory. Despite the early hour he looked freshly showered and shaved, and very sharp in his well-cut suit. "Revisiting the scene of your crimes?"

"Not funny," Avery said, bristling. She pulled free of Alex and stepped up to Newton, sick of his bullying tone. She wanted to slap him. "We haven't committed a crime."

"Here for a visit, were you?" he said, his eyes narrowing suspiciously as he eyed them all in turn. His gaze lingered on Briar. "I haven't met you yet, but I think you own the potion shop."

"It is not a potion shop!" Briar said, almost spitting. Wow, Newton had a real knack for getting under their skin.

"Let me introduce DI Newton and Officer Moore," Avery said, gesturing with a flourish.

"Newton?" Briar repeated, puzzled. She looked as if she was about to say more, when Newton interrupted.

"Now that you're here, I'd like your opinion on what happened in the museum."

"Why?" Alex asked immediately. He had also stepped closer to Newton, as if challenging him.

"Calm down, Bonneville. I just want your opinion. And I'll get your alibis later. Wait here," he said, as he stalked off into the museum, Moore close behind him.

"Alibis!" Avery huffed, feeling like she wanted to rip Newton's head off. "Why should we need to provide an alibi? He clearly wants to blame us for anything and everything! That supercilious bastard."

"But what if the demons have attacked again?" El asked, worried. "What if someone else is dead because of us?"

Alex shook his head and sat on the stone wall that edged the car park. "Not because of us. We didn't cause this. We didn't summon demons."

Avery was too annoyed to sit, so she paced restlessly. "Who is out there, doing this? We need to find them!"

"We need to do lots of things," El said wearily.

Briar was sitting quietly on the wall next to Alex, but she finally broke her silence. "Is the name Newton familiar to you?"

"Er, the DI?" Alex asked, looking at Briar as if she'd gone mad.

"No! I mean, other than him. I've read the name somewhere."

Avery now felt her annoyance turning to Briar. "Haven't we got other things to be worried about?"

Briar looked at her, ignoring her tone. "It's an old name in this town, isn't it?"

"It's not an uncommon name anywhere," Alex said. "Besides, lots of people have lived here for years."

Briar looked perplexed. "I think I know the name from some of that info we got from Anne. I think he's from one of the *old* families."

Avery glanced at the other two, and was relieved to find they looked as confused as she felt. "Briar, please explain. It's too early, and my brain's full of other crap."

Briar remained unruffled by Avery's sarcasm. "I mean the old families with *magic.*"

El laughed. "What! Newton and magic?"

"He might not have magical abilities, but I'm sure his ancestors have."

"It might explain why he's anti-witch, and has an unhealthy interest in our habits," Alex said.

Their conversation was broken by a shout. They looked around to see Newton beckoning them from the open door.

"Yes, sir," Avery muttered under her breath as they walked over.

"I'm breaking protocol by letting you in, so don't touch anything!" he ordered. Without another word he headed inside, and they followed him in.

The inside of the museum was lit by the unnatural glare of overhead lights. The windows were small and let in only a small amount of daylight. Small, yellow spotlights lit up the displays, and Avery presumed that would normally be the only light source when visitors were here.

For a few seconds Avery gazed around the museum, taking in the numerous displays in glass cabinets, both against the walls and in the middle of the floor. They were filled with old maps, manuscripts, and lots of other objects, but her attention was swiftly drawn by a display that had been smashed, and on the wall was a large, complex sigel written in what looked like dried blood. Avery felt her skin prickle as she recognised it and all her annoyance at Newton drained out of her.

She could sense the power from the sign, and all four them had stopped in the middle of the room.

Newton stood next to the sign, looking at them curiously. "So, what is it?" he asked.

Alex spoke first, and he walked closer to the display. "It's an ancient ward, essentially a warning to stay away."

That was an understatement, Avery thought. She swallowed her fear and joined him, with El and Briar close behind.

Newton looked sceptical. "Really? Because you have all gone very pale. Now is not a good time to be holding something back."

Alex glanced at her, a questioning look on his face, and she felt something shift within her. This wasn't a time to be keeping secrets, and Alex knew it, too.

Avery looked at Newton, trying to gauge his reaction. "It marks a doorway, and within it is a warning to stay away. It essentially says this place is claimed."

To give him credit, Newton wasn't at all fazed by that statement. Instead, he narrowed his eyes and folded his arms across his broad chest. "A doorway to what? And claimed by who?"

"A doorway to another dimension. One in which unnatural, non-human forms live. And it is claimed by whoever made the sign."

"How does the doorway work?"

"I can't speak for the others, but I don't know how it works. I just know what it is. But it's powerful, I can sense that."

Newton looked at them one by one, as if trying to read their minds. "I'll rephrase the question. It's a doorway, you say. Will it open? Or is it just some gimmicky sign that someone with a weird sense of humour has put up."

"In theory," Avery said, "if you say the right words, it will open."

"And then what?"

"It will allow things—*beings*—to pass through to our dimension. And back again. But no human would ever survive there."

"So it's more for something to come through?"

"Yes. But someone may be taken through as a type of... sacrifice." Avery could scarcely believe she'd said that.

Newton's tone changed, and he ran his hand through his hair, looking worried. "The cleaner's missing. There's blood in the kitchen, and blood in that sign. Could something have taken the cleaner through there?"

Avery felt sick. "Maybe, yes. But Newton, you have to understand—we don't do this. I know you don't like us for our interest in the esoteric and natural magic, but this—" she gestured towards the sign. "I really don't know how this works, only the theory."

Alex was looking at the destroyed display, the glass smashed and the objects beneath it scattered. "How do you know the cleaner is missing? He could have had an accident and gone to the hospital."

"There's far too much blood there for anyone to have survived. Haven't you noticed the blood?" He pointed at the floor, and for the first time, Avery saw the smear of blood that ran from the door at the back to under the sign, and beneath the musty smell, she could detect the sharp, metallic odour of blood. "There's more in the kitchen."

"But who called you?" Alex asked.

"The lady who manages the place on Sundays. She's out the back with Moore. She's in shock and we need to get her out of here, but I wanted your opinion first."

"What was in the display?" El asked.

"You'd better come and ask her. I'll take you around the long way—I don't want you walking in anything." Newton headed back across the museum and they trailed after him as he led them around the back of the building to the kitchen and storage area.

Moore was sitting in a small stock room with a uniformed police officer and an older lady who sat on a stool, looking tearful and clutching a cup of tea in a paper cup that someone must have gone to fetch her. A doorway showed a glimpse of the kitchen, and Avery saw a lot of blood on the floor and splashed up the walls. She shuddered.

Newton put his hand on the lady's shoulder. "I'm sorry Mrs Gray," he said, gently, in a tone Avery had never heard him use before. "I need to ask you another question. I have some people here who I've asked to help." He nodded towards them. "What was in the display that was destroyed?"

She looked at them, clearly bewildered by the turn her day was taking. "It was a display about the Witchfinder and his visit to White Haven back in the 16th century. There are also some things relating to Helena, the witch who was burned here years before." She looked at Avery sadly. "Sorry, my dear, I know she was your ancestor."

Avery experienced a moment of shock. She hadn't realised anyone outside of their circle had connected her to Helena. She was amazed this woman could show any compassion, considering what she'd witnessed in the kitchen. She thought she'd be accusing her, not sympathising.

"Was there anything new in the display, Mrs Gray?" Briar asked, surprising them all. She was normally so quiet.

The old woman shook her head. "No. That display has been like that for years."

Newton interrupted. "Any other questions? I'd like to take Mrs Gray to the station now, for her statement."

"No, thank you." Alex answered for all of them.

"I need a few more words with Mrs Gray. Can you wait outside for a minute?"

It wasn't really a request, and they filed out, blinking in the warm sunshine. Avery felt as if she'd been in a cave and had forgotten it was a beautiful summer morning. She headed to the stone wall that looked over the harbour and sat down, vaguely aware of the others next to her.

The harbour was filled with boats grounded on the sand. The tide was edging out, and pools of water gathered in the sand beneath the harbour wall. The sound of gulls mixed with the passing of cars and the occasional barking dog. Everything seemed so normal.

"Do you think the cleaner has really gone?" Briar asked. She sat next to Avery, her hands clasped in her lap.

"Yes," Alex answered. "I don't think they'll ever find a body."

"We need to seal that doorway," El said. She was pacing backwards and forwards. "If we leave it open, it can keep coming back. It's right in the middle of the town!"

"How do we seal it?" Alex asked, annoyed. "I haven't even seen one before, except in illustrations."

Avery thought about the books she had in the store and in her attic. "I have some old books about necromancy. I'll look as soon as we get back. What about you two? You have the oldest grimoires. Is there anything in them?"

El shook her head, bewildered. "I don't know. I've barely begun to look at it. I'll check it as soon as I get in."

"Well, you know there are demon and spirit related spells in mine, but I'm inexperienced when it comes to that type of magic, and if I'm honest, I've avoided studying them," Alex said. He looked across the car park to the museum. "They'll surely close the museum. I guess we won't see inside there again."

"I can't believe Newton let us in at all!" Avery said.

The sound of a door slamming made them turn. The uniformed officer and Moore were escorting Mrs Gray to a police car, and Newton was heading their way.

He stood in front of them, looking far calmer than Avery felt. Maybe he was just better at holding it together than them. He smoothed his tie down, patted his pocket, and brought out a packet of cigarettes. He swiftly took one out and lit it, inhaling deeply.

"So," he said, watching them carefully, "What are we going to do about that doorway?"

Avery looked at Newton with new appreciation. He said '*we*' and he didn't argue with the notion of the other dimensions or beings. "You're not going to arrest us, then?"

"Not unless I find your fingerprints everywhere. SOCO's on the way now," he said, referring to scene of crime investigators. "And if it reassures you to hear me say it, I don't think you're murderers, anyway."

Briar still sat next to Avery, watching the exchange. "You're one of *those* Newtons, aren't you?"

Newton took another long drag on his cigarette and exhaled slowly. "What do you mean by *those* Newtons?"

"There are several old families in this town, Detective. We know some of them have a more diverse history than others. I'm pretty sure you do, too. And your family is one of them."

"I'm aware of my personal history, Briar," he said softly. "I stay away from it. But yes, I know all about it, and about you, too. It's my business to know. And I know it wasn't an animal that attacked that woman the other night, either. What's going on?" He watched her intently, his eyes sweeping across her face.

Avery had the distinct impression that this was a test of honesty. Of trust. He was gauging how much he could trust them, and they were wondering the same about him.

"Honestly," Briar said, "we really don't know. But we know someone wants something badly enough to call on any type of help they can."

"You're lying—all of you. You know more than that. But that's okay. You'll tell me eventually. I just hope it's before there are more deaths, because whatever's happening here, you're probably the only ones who can stop it." He took one final drag from his cigarette and threw it on the pavement. "You have my number. Call me when you decide to help."

Sixteen

Avery sat in a cafe around the corner from the museum with a large coffee and a plate of bacon, eggs, and toast in front of her. She sipped at her coffee appreciatively, wishing there was brandy in it.

"My day is not turning out the way I'd planned," Avery said, in between mouthfuls of food.

"That cleaner's isn't, either," Alex replied. He'd ordered a full breakfast, and Avery was amazed at the speed with which he was putting it away.

"Cheers, Alex. I was trying not to think about that."

"That's all I can think about," Briar spoke up. She was picking at her toast. "I keep smelling that blood."

El had ordered a large slice of chocolate cake with her coffee. "As soon as I've finished this, I'm off to look at my new grimoire." She lowered her voice conspiratorially. "We have to at least find a spell that will prevent whatever comes out of that doorway from going any further."

"I've been thinking about that," Avery said. "We could use a protective circle like we cast last night."

"It needs to be stronger," El said, dipping some cake in her coffee. "That wouldn't have lasted long. And we're not going to be there when it comes back. I hope."

"We have to find out who's causing this," Briar said. "I wonder how Gil and Reuben are getting on?"

Alex pushed his plate away. "Better than we are, I hope! Anyway, I'd better go. I'm on the lunchtime shift. I'll call you later," he said to Avery as he pushed his chair back, and then he disappeared out the door.

Avery watched him go, wondering what his final comment meant. *Was there something more to, "I'll call you?"* When she turned back to the table, El and Briar were looking at her speculatively.

El broke the silence. "He'll call you?" She grinned. "Is there something going on we should know about?"

"No! I presume he just wants to know if we've made progress later." Avery sounded evasive and lame. She picked up her coffee in the hope that someone would change the subject.

Briar shook her head, a sad smile on her face. "No, I don't think so, Avery. That's a different 'I'll call you.' He said it with *meaning*."

"Oh, yeah. There was definitely meaning there," El agreed, smirking.

Avery gave her a hard stare and then looked at Briar. "Er, Briar, you can tell me to butt out, but do you like Alex, or something like that?" *Wow. How sad was that?* She sounded like a schoolgirl.

"Something like that," Briar admitted, still picking at her now very cold toast. "But it's not going to happen. I think he's way more interested in you." She shrugged. "Win some, lose some."

Now Avery felt like crap. She didn't know Briar very well, and hadn't spent much time with her until this week, but she liked her, and for some inexplicable reason now felt really guilty. "Well, nothing has really happened. He's just a flirt, and he likes to keep his options open."

El shook her head. "I disagree. He acts the flirt, but I don't think he is, not really."

Avery grunted and decided it was time to change the subject. "Whatever. What do you think of Newton?"

"He looks good in his suit," El said, grinning.

"But he smokes!" Briar grimaced into her toast.

"No, he's *smoking*!" El countered. "Anyway. I also need to go. Avery, you need to come up with a better protection spell. I hear you're good at that sort of thing. What about you, Briar?"

"I need to prepare some stock for the shop, and then more research." She looked back at Avery. "If you can, get that spell prepared for tonight—we need to secure that doorway."

"You mean, break in to the museum?" Avery asked, shocked.

"Or, we could call DI Newton," Briar said, grinning. "He wants to help."

Avery opened the door of her flat and took a deep breath of relief at being home. She was lucky she had Sally as her manager and Dan to help out, or she wouldn't have as much freedom to pursue hunts for hidden grimoires. The last few days had been a whirlwind of action, revelation and danger. She did, however, need time on her own, and on Sundays the bookshop remained closed.

In one week her entire life seemed to have changed. While she had always enjoyed her magical skills, her magic was always benign. This was how it should be. She tended her garden, harvested ingredients, read books on the subject, and tested her abilities. She had hundreds of dried herbs prepared, access to fresh ones, and she liked to try new spells. She didn't know how Alex had known, but he was right. She got that from her grandmother. And yes, there was Alex. The other night their kiss had been unexpected, but not unwelcome. If she was honest, she really wasn't sure what she thought about it. And she had no idea what he thought; he hadn't said anything, other than the enigmatic—*I'll call you*.

She decided that before she did anything else, she would clean the flat. The mundane occupation would help her process things. For the next hour, she vacuumed, tidied, and polished. The cats either scooted out of her way or watched inquisitively.

When she'd finished, she headed through the gate and into her garden. The energies of the previous night had settled, but she still sensed the disturbance that the demons had brought. She followed the winding gravel paths until she reached the grassed area at the centre. Briar had done well. The grass was back in place and as smooth as a bowling green. In fact, it looked better than it had before. The plants from the surrounding beds were tucked back into the soil, and apart from a few damaged stems, looked none the worse for their ordeal. It was hard to recall the horror of the previous night, standing here in the bright warm sunshine. She suddenly recalled Briar's advice about water, so she pulled the hose from the shed and then turned it on the borders.

The events of last night were so confusing; she couldn't say where the demons had come from. It seemed that they had arrived as soon as she had opened the door of their protective circle and the ravens had flown free. *Ravens*. That was an interesting bird to have manifested from the box. They were bringers of news, dark omens, and wisdom. *What a mix.*

She could only presume that the demons had been waiting some-where in another dimension for a manifestation, or some sign of magical activity, and had attacked as soon as the birds were released. It would have taken a huge amount of power to control them.

Avery finished watering the plants, turned off the hose, and then lay on the grass and closed her eyes, thinking again of last night. Could anything *else* have been there? She couldn't sense anything at the time. Maybe the witch who was hunting them had been above them, spirit walking. Or had at least been above the town, waiting and watching for a magical disturbance. Alex hadn't been sure what had attacked them before, but maybe the witch controlled demons both in the spirit dimension and the material. Whoever they were was one step ahead of them. She laughed to herself. *No, they were several steps ahead.* They needed to do a lot of catching up.

The doorway to the other dimension in the museum was an unexpected development. She wondered if this was an easier way to control the demons. Manifesting out of the air must take a lot of control. Creating a doorway would require less energy. Well, once the initial sacrifice had been made. Two people were dead. Two too many. The sunlight played across her face, and it was tempting to sleep, but there was too much to do. She opened her eyes, gazing at the sky above. It was a deep, endless blue, with just a few clouds scudding by. Someone, somewhere would be mourning a loved one.

They had to seal that doorway. *Did their adversary presume they were so weak that they couldn't defend the town? That they didn't care?* She was determined to prove them wrong. She leapt to her feet, her energy renewed. It was time to prepare.

Avery sat at her worktable in the attic and pulled out several old books she had on necromancy, spreading them in front of her. They were filled with diagrams of circles of protection, summonings, invocations, and lists of the type of demons that could be summoned and what they could be used for. The diagrams were complex and she felt her heart growing heavy at the mere thought of doing them. She saw an image that looked familiar and reached for her own spell book.

Her grimoire was filled with spells, all written by different hands through the years. The first spells were written in ink, and there were blots and splashes in places, while others had been written meticulously. Some spells were illustrated, with pictures of herbs, roots, and images of the moon. There were spells she knew by heart because she used them regularly, but there were others that she hardly used or ever looked at. The more modern spells were written in ballpoint pen, and she had annotated several spells that she had tested and found needed improving. These she had rewritten, and there were many pages filled with her own handwriting of reworked spells and new ones.

But there were spells at the back that she hardly ever looked at. These spells came with a warning. Magic should never be used to harm, but many of the spells in the back of the grimoire were for exactly that purpose. There were warped love spells, spells to bind, to silence, to dull the wits, to confuse, to bring bad fortune, to cause infertility, and many others. And there were spells to control and summon spirits. While this didn't really include demons, she assumed the principles would be the same.

Avery turned the pages slowly, making notes, and ran through several scenarios in her head, testing out protection spells until she had something she thought would work. She grabbed her cutting knife and headed to her borders. She needed roots and fresh leaves—catnip, peppermint, chamomile, geranium, Solomon's seal, garlic. And she needed fresh seaweed; she would have to go to the beach. Some plants would need harvesting at dusk, but she could begin some preparations now. Of her dried plants, she would need mandrake, foxglove, and rose hips. She needed to make two potions.

While she worked, she wondered if it would be worth phoning her grandmother. She was in a home now, her mind a shadow of its former self. But of all her family members still living, she had the best knowledge of witchcraft. Her mother had walked away from it and White Haven, and her sister had quickly followed, leaving her alone. Her father had long gone, unnerved by the family legacy. But Avery couldn't deny her blood and had remained, working her magic alone. She shook her head. No, she couldn't disturb her grandmother. She had to do this on her own, but maybe, after tonight, she would visit her, and ask her what she remembered about the Jacksons.

Once she had what she needed, she headed back to her workroom and started to prepare her ingredients. She lost herself in the work as she meticulously chopped and ground the herbs, saying the necessary words. Circe and Medea watched her all afternoon until she had finished. Avery petted them and then headed down to the kitchen to feed them. She heard the thundering of their paws as they jumped off the table and followed her to the kitchen.

Once she'd fed them she grabbed an oilskin bag and headed to the beach. It was time to get the seaweed and make the potion.

Avery eased her van to a stop on the car park overlooking the deserted beach. The cove was virtually empty, as she'd expected. It was about fifteen minutes outside White Haven, and access to the cove was down a long, winding path from the cliff top.

She had chosen to come here because there wouldn't be too many people to see her small rituals as she picked up seaweed. As much as she loved White Haven, on a bright day like this, the harbour and surrounding beaches would be full of families and children.

A cool wind blew in from the sea, and she wrapped her cardigan around her as her long skirt buffeted around her ankles. When she arrived on the beach, she kicked off her flip-flops and put them in her bag, feeling the damp sand underfoot as she made her way to the shore. In the far distance she could see a man walking his dog, but otherwise the beach was deserted.

Avery headed to the rock pools, looking for seaweed still attached to the rocks. She trod carefully, and finding what she needed, brought her cutting knife out, its silver blade flashing in the light, and whispered the necessary invocation as she cut the seaweed free and put it in her bag. She wandered to the far edge of the beach where the cliff stretched into the sea, enjoying the silence, and watched the man head up the rickety wooden steps, the dog prancing around his ankles, and then he was gone and she was alone.

In a sheltered spot, out of the breeze, Avery piled up some driftwood and uttered a simple spell to create fire. She brought out her small, blackened cauldron and placed it among the flames, adding saltwater and chopping the seaweed into it. For a few minutes she watched, and when it was time, she added some of the other herbs she had brought with her. Passing her hands over the mixture she said the spell that would bind them together.

There. It was done. Wrapping a cloth around her hands, she took the small bowl out of the flames and put it on the sand to cool, and then stopped for moment. She had heard a noise. A soft sound, like a call on the breeze.

Avery stood and looked across the beach and up at the cliffs, but no one was in sight. And then she heard her name floating on the wind. She jumped, and a shiver passed through her. *Who was that?*

The voice grew louder and stronger, like a seagull crying on the wind. It came closer and closer, but there was still no one in sight. She grounded herself, preparing for whatever may come next.

Without warning, a man appeared on the sand a short distance away. He was tall and dressed in black, his dark hair short, and he strode quickly towards her. Her heart started thudding and she raised her hands. If demons appeared now, she was toast. She looked around, but there was nowhere to run. The crags of the coast were at her back, and rock pools lay between her and the sea.

She turned back to him, keeping her energy raised and ready to strike.

He stopped when he was a few feet away, allowing her to see his features clearly. He was older than her. Early forties, maybe. His dark hair was streaked with grey, and his pale blue eyes fixed on her intensely as he took in her every detail.

She found her voice. "Who are you?"

He laughed. "I'm one of you, Avery."

"What does that mean?" she asked, already annoyed.

"From one of the old families."

"Well, most people I know don't manifest out of thin air, so that doesn't surprise me. But which family?"

He laughed, showing even white teeth against his tanned skin. "I like your spirit, Avery, but then again all of the women in your family have a certain boldness."

She glared at him, not liking to be on the back foot. He was an arrogant prick on a monumental scale. "Excellent, so glad I meet your approval. I presume all of the men in *your* family have a similar streak of dickishness." She was being deliberately prevocational in order to wipe the arrogant smile off his face. It didn't work.

"My, my. How polite you are."

"Oh, cut the crap. I presume you're the one responsible for the demons?"

He smiled, but it didn't reach his eyes. "Maybe. I'm here to offer you a warning, before anyone gets hurt."

"Too late. Two people are already dead."

He shrugged. "Not our people."

"They were still people!" She was incensed and wanted nothing better than to strike him, but she knew that would be pointless. She had no idea how he'd appeared out of thin air, which meant he was clearly more powerful than her.

"Forget them, Avery. You need to think about you, Alex, Briar, Gil, Elspeth, and Reuben. You are in possession of things we need. We don't want to hurt you to get them, but we will, if we have to."

Her blood ran cold. He knew them all. "Can we skip the cryptic messages? What do you want?"

"The grimoires, of course."

"But they're not yours. They belong to us."

"To be blunt, you don't deserve them. You've let your powers grow weak." He looked at her in disappointment.

"Well, maybe now we have a chance to grow stronger again." She was making empty threats and he knew it, but she wasn't going to be walked over. And the more she stood there, the more she knew she wanted her grimoire. Now that she knew they existed, it had tripped a desire that she couldn't switch off.

"And maybe *we* have a chance to grow stronger." He tipped his head to the side, watching her reaction.

"No. Absolutely not. They're ours."

He sighed. "I'm not sure you should answer on behalf of everyone else. Ask them. They may disagree. I can take possession of Elspeth's and Alex's as soon as they are ready."

She thought for a moment. She was pretty sure Alex and El would tell him to get lost, but Gil or Briar? And then another thought struck her. If he was more powerful than them, why couldn't he just take them? Breaching their protection spells could be easy for him. *Maybe there was a reason he couldn't?*

"I'll ask them. But don't get excited. May I tell them who called today?" she asked with an exaggerated politeness through gritted teeth.

"Caspian Faversham. I'm not sure Anne will have heard of me," he said with a smirk.

And then he disappeared in a swirl of air and sea spray, and Avery was left alone on the beach.

Seventeen

As soon as Avery was back in White Haven, her mobile phone rang. It was Briar, and she sounded excited.

"Avery, I got hold of Newton, and he agreed."

"Agreed to what?" she asked, trying to pull into the side of the road while she spoke. She still felt flustered by her encounter on the beach.

"To let us into the museum."

Avery was silent for a moment, dumbfounded. She hadn't really thought Briar would call him, and she certainly didn't expect him to agree. "Are you kidding? I mean, you actually asked him?"

"I said I would. I told him we would try to close the doorway, and he agreed."

"Wow. I did not expect that." She gazed out of her window at the traffic which snaked its way through the narrow streets in the centre of the town. Sundays did not make the place any less busy. "What time?"

"Late. After midnight. But can we do it?" Briar sounded worried. "I mean, have you got a spell ready?"

"I have something that may work, but I'd like to see if El or Alex have had any luck."

"Alex is working, remember?"

Avery exhaled slowly. "I forgot. Look, Briar, I met someone on the beach, and he threatened us."

"Are you all right? What happened? Who was it?" she asked in a breathless race.

"I'm fine. He materialised out of thin air, and he's called Caspian Faversham. It's a stupid name." She snorted, glad she could ridicule him in some way.

"Who the hell is that?"

"I have no idea. Look, I can't talk now, I'm parked precariously. Come around to mine later, and I'll explain everything. And we can talk through the spell I've tweaked."

Briar was silent for a moment. "I'm not sure I can cope with demons again."

"I'm not sure I can either, so we better seal that doorway."

Avery returned to her worktable in the attic, and this time spread Anne's research around her. The need to find her own old grimoire was now more urgent than ever. There was no way that she would let Faversham get it.

Anne had been rigorous in her documentation. Her family tree was exhaustive and fascinating. It was strange to see her family line travelling back so many generations. Her finger ran across the paper as she focussed on old names, all of them unfamiliar except for the most recent and Helena; her name was a beacon for all the wrong reasons. She could kick herself for not going to the museum sooner.

And what if Briar was right? What if Newton was from another old family who had abandoned their witchcraft and their place in the town history? What did this mean about the DI? It seemed he knew more than he wanted to say. Any normal person would have scoffed at supposed doorways to another dimension, but he didn't blink. And moreover, who was Caspian Faversham? And were there others they had no idea about? What did these old grimoires *really* hide? She sighed. *So many questions.* Avery thought she knew the history of White Haven, and her place in it, but now she sensed there was a lot that had been hidden.

She soon abandoned Anne's histories, and instead pulled a couple of books towards her that described the history of White Haven. They were small imprints, written by local authors. One was only a few years old, and the other had been written decades ago.

She looked at the most recent. The cover had a black and white photo of White Haven on it. She skimmed the contents. It seemed the book described the history of the town from the Doomsday records, but a lot of the content was on the witch trials, and then progressed on to the smuggling in the later centuries—the Cornish coast was renowned for it—before it reached the present. She flicked to the back cover and found a picture of the author, an older man named Samuel Kingston, and wondered if he still lived locally. She'd check later.

She glanced at her watch. She'd text Alex and El about meeting later; she was sure they'd be around to help. But for now, everything she needed for the spell was prepared. She could finally relax and read.

Avery roused later from a light sleep, stretched out on the old sofa, her book on the floor. Shadows were creeping across the room, the temperature had dropped, and her stomach was uncomfortably empty.

She headed down to the kitchen to heat some soup and thought about what she'd learned from the history book. It seemed the

Witchfinder General had come searching for several locals who were renowned as *cunning folk*—the term used for those who helped their local communities through pagan beliefs and healing. Although they were generally respected, when hysteria started to sweep the villages, fear superseded rational thought and a few were accused of witchcraft. Kingston mentioned the names of several women and men who had been interrogated, but she only recognised a couple. Helena's, and the surname Jackson, which she presumed must be Gil's ancestor. According to the records, two locals had been drowned through the testing of their witch abilities—if you survived the attempted drowning you were condemned as a witch anyway, and Helena was burned at the stake.

Avery was embarrassed by how little she knew about the actual facts of the investigations. All she'd really known about was Helena. She had no idea about the drowning tests. And disappointingly, there was no name of Faversham in the records, or Newton, for that matter. Kingston must have had access to all the records of the trials, and she wondered if she could access them, too. Maybe there was more he hadn't published; more names that could explain what had happened. Avery still couldn't believe that Helena wouldn't have used her powers to escape, despite what Alex said about saving the others. Something just didn't add up.

She sighed, frustrated, and took her soup and toast to the sofa and switched on the TV. She needed a distraction, something normal. Unfortunately, she found the news. There was a local report about the break-in at the museum and the cleaner's disappearance. At least there was no mention of sorcery and doorways to other dimensions. The trouble was, would it stay hidden?

There was a knock at the door, disturbing her musing, and she found El outside, looking determined.

"Are you okay?" Avery asked, as she welcomed her in.

El slung her heavy backpack onto the sofa. "That grimoire is baffling, amazing, and frustrating. I've already found out so much that I could use in my metal work, but there's stuff I need time to get my head around. And," she paused, looking at Avery as if wondering how to phrase what she was going to say next.

"Go on," Avery said. "I have a feeling things are going to get a lot weirder around here."

"Well, I now have spells to summon demons and spirits, specifically to help work with metals and fire. I'm pretty freaked out." She looked around the room. "Have you got beer?"

"Sure," Avery said, her heart sinking a little as she headed to the fridge and pulled out two bottles. She popped the caps off and handed one to El. "If I'm honest, I was expecting this. It seems there was a lot of magic our ancestors used that we're not comfortable with now. Necromancy was common in the medieval period. And it was all in Latin. The church condemned it, and yet the priests controlled it."

"But I really didn't expect to find this in our family grimoires." El took a swig of beer and leaned on the counter, her long hair falling forward and framing her face.

"I think we all have to expect it." And then Avery had a thought. "Hey, this is actually really good timing, El. I've been working on a spell to seal the doorway. Those spells in your grimoire could help—although I think I have one that will work. Have you brought it with you?"

"Sure, it's in there," she said, nodding towards her pack. "Briar told me what we're doing later. Have a look."

Avery put her beer down and gently pulled the grimoire out, putting it on the counter between them. She couldn't help but grin. "Wow, El, this is so cool! I mean, look at it!"

The leather cover was dark brown, and a triangle, the sign for the fire element, was burnt into the centre of the cover. Avery ran her hand over the leather, marvelling at how soft it felt, worn over the years by thousands of hands. She looked at El. "I'm jealous. I want to find mine."

El smiled encouragingly. "You will. I'll help."

Avery turned the pages made of old, thick paper, the handwriting changing as the owners had over the years. The language of the early spells was difficult to decipher, and some were in Latin. She found the spells about summoning demons early in the book, written by the witches from the medieval times. The drawings were complex, but made carefully and precisely. There were pictures of pentagrams, circles, double circles, inverse pentagrams, and invocations, all with instructions beneath them.

Avery took a deep breath and exhaled slowly, looking at El. "Wow. Again. Let's go upstairs, compare it to what I have, and see what you think of my spell. Although, I'm not planning to mess with the doorway. I just want to seal it into a protection circle."

"Sure," El said, gathering up the book. "I'm going to call Gil and Reuben about tonight, if that's okay. Strength in numbers."

Avery nodded. "With luck, we'll seal the doorway and won't see any demons at all."

The museum stood dark and forbidding that night, and the group sheltered in the shadows of the back wall. Police tape sealed the front and rear entrances, and the only sound around them was the crashing of the waves against the sea wall.

They had parked up the road, out of sight, and walked down, immediately heading to the back of the building where they couldn't be seen by the casual pedestrian.

Alex looked at them and grinned. "Is this ninja witch night?"

Briar shivered, despite the warm night air. "I don't feel like a ninja."

"I don't either, but I'll do my best," Reuben said, from where he stood next to El, his silhouette lean and tall.

Avery looked at them, and despite her nerves, had to laugh. They were all dressed in black—black tops, black jeans, and boots, and everyone with long hair had tied it back. Reuben and El had even pulled black hats over their bright, light hair. She looked at Alex. "Well, we do need to be discrete."

"Even with a police escort? Where is he, anyway?" he asked, referring to Newton.

"He'll be here soon," Briar assured them.

"I'm not sure I even like the guy," Gil said. "He could arrest us after this." Gil had been reluctant to come, thinking the whole thing felt like a trap.

"I'm not sure there are laws about prosecuting witches anymore," Alex reasoned. "Anyway, here he comes."

They looked across the car park and saw the tall figure of Newton approaching. When he reached them, they could see he had come dressed in similar clothing to them—the suit had gone. He looked more approachable in his casual clothes, and his short hair was ruffled.

He glanced at them all, but spoke to Briar. "Thanks for the call. You did the right thing."

"We're not murderers, Newton, despite what you think of our beliefs," she said, a hint of annoyance in her voice.

Gil stepped forward, his face grim. He was shorter than Newton, but he looked up at him, meeting his stare. "Forgive my disbelief, but the police don't normally encourage magic on the site of a murder. In fact, the police, like the general public, usually refuse to believe in magic at all."

Newton's face was implacable, especially in the dark. All Avery could see were the firm lines of his cheeks and chin, and a dark glimmer in his eyes. "Well, I'm not most police, and I certainly don't want any more deaths in White Haven. Are we going to get on with it?"

Gil remained silent, trying to assess Newton, but Alex answered. "Yes, let's get it over with."

"Have you got what you need?"

"Yes," Avery answered. "It's all in my pack, and Briar's."

Newton nodded and led them to the back door, pulling away the police tape and taking a key from his pocket. Avery watched him as he turned the key, opened the door and listened for a moment, then stepped inside and gestured to them to wait.

Avery swallowed nervously, her heart pounding, hoping he'd return and that something wasn't already lurking. The wait seemed to last forever, but then he was back, calling them inside, and they shuffled in after him, the last one in shutting the door behind them.

The inside of the museum was pitch black, other than the broad beams of their torches, and Newton led the way into the main room. "Watch the floor. The blood's still here, but it's dried now. And don't go in the kitchen."

Avery glanced in there as she passed and saw there was a large pool of congealed blood still on the floor. The smell was stronger than ever, and she stepped quickly past the opening, focusing only on what she needed to do.

Once in the main room, she looked around, assessing the space and where best to position themselves. She looked at the archaic symbols drawn on the wall with renewed interest now that she had been studying others like it all afternoon. There were similarities, but also strong differences. It looked even more menacing than she remembered.

"So, what's the plan?" Newton asked.

"We have no idea how to close the doorway," Avery said, "so we can't prevent anything from coming through. But, we do know how to make a powerful protective circle around it, and we can make a devil's trap within it."

"A what? I thought this thing let demons and spirits in?" Newton asked, his eyes narrowing.

"It's called a devil's trap, but essentially it will trap any spirit, ghost, or demon form that comes through there. In theory."

"So, it might not work?"

Alex rolled his eyes. "Well, it's not something we do every day, Newton, so no, we're not sure."

"But you *are* witches?" he confirmed, his arms crossed as he looked at them.

Avery felt the knot in her stomach intensify. This was a subject they'd been dancing around with Newton.

"Yes," El finally said, looking him squarely in the eye. "Good ones. And by that I mean good in intent. But we're not as powerful as whoever made that."

"What were you doing up at Hawk House the other night?" he asked.

"None of your business," El snapped.

"I'm just going to get on with preparing everything," Avery said jumping in, and placed her bag on the floor, well away from the blood and the area they were going to seal.

Alex and Briar bent down next to her while the argument and inter-rogation about the other night continued. She pulled out a selection of candles, incense, her chalice, cauldron, the chosen herbs, and the potion she had made earlier.

Briar fetched a huge bag of salt from her bag and Avery's grimoire. "Here you go, Avery. I'll mark out the circle." She walked off and left her with Alex.

"So, how are you feeling?" Alex asked, watching her. He sat on the floor, his presence unexpectedly calming.

"I'm okay. Getting used to dealing with demons, I guess." She looked up at him, and he held her gaze.

"You should come over to my place later. There's safety in numbers."

Avery's heart immediately started racing, but instead she said, "Er, yes, maybe."

He looked slightly nonplussed. "Maybe?"

"You're distracting me, and I need to concentrate," she said, looking away and feeling flushed. *Was she suddenly fourteen again?*

"I make a great breakfast," he said, still watching her with a speculative look on his face and the hint of a grin. "But I'm serious. There's safety in numbers, and there's a lot of crap happening."

She smiled, but it faltered as she thought of her encounter on the beach. "I know. And there's something I need to share with all of you later. Something that happened earlier."

"What?" he asked, his grin disappearing.

"Later. We need to get this done."

He sighed. "All right. Now, tell me what we need to do again."

Avery had already outlined the spell she'd planned, but she went over it again before pulling another old book on necromancy from her bag. She flicked through it until she found a picture of a pentagram surrounded by a double circle, filled with images and runes. "This is the devil's trap. We need to draw it on the floor under the doorway."

"What with? Please don't say blood."

"A mixture of my own design." She pulled a dark bottle out of her bag that was stoppered with a cork and cupped it gently, a warm glow suffusing out of her hands and into the potion in the bottle. She said a few words quietly under her breath, and the light increased, even as she passed it to Alex. "There you go. I'll be with you in a minute—don't start it yet!"

He leapt to his feet, taking the bottle and the necromancy book with him. Avery called over to El, Gil, and Reuben, who were still arguing with Newton. "Hey, guys. We need to prepare the room. Here are some candles, and we need them placed at certain points."

The arguing stopped immediately and they placed the candles as instructed, while Briar placed some just outside the large salt semi-circle she had made that touched the walls on either side of the dimensional doorway.

While they were getting the room ready, Avery prepared the altar on the floor within the semi-circle, and she saw Newton watching. "Are you sure you don't want to leave?"

"No. I need to see this."

"But nothing will happen, hopefully. At least nothing will come out of that doorway."

"You don't know that."

She sighed. "No, I don't. Something may come out of it right now, and then we'll all be in trouble. But you know more about this than you're letting on."

He remained silent.

"Now who's being stubborn?" She looked around at the others. "Are we ready?"

They nodded and she turned back to Newton. "Stay back—whatever happens."

Alex stood ready to begin marking out the trap, the dimensional doorway looming over him. The rest lined up along the inner edge of the salt circle, the altar in front of them. Avery recited the spell line by line, the others repeating it. She felt the energy in the room start to rise as Alex daubed the floor with the mixture she'd given him, copying the trap carefully and precisely.

It took some time to complete, and as they continued to chant the spell, the air crackled with power and the complex design of the trap glowed in the muted light.

As soon as Alex had completed the final outer circle, he stepped back to meet the others, their hands linking as he joined them in the spell, and their voices rose on the air as if they had developed a life of their own.

There was one final step Avery needed to complete, and she reached for the bowl containing the other herb spell mixture she had brought, looking up at the complex shapes and runes of the doorway. It pulsed with a dark power that emanated from whatever was beyond; she could feel it far more acutely now. She sensed its malevolence and an age-old evil that was unlike anything else she'd experienced. When she started this spell, a large part of her was worried, fearful even. It was so different from anything she had done before, but now as the power of the others flooded through her, she felt excited at what they could do together. They were far more powerful than Faversham realised.

While the others continued to chant, Avery daubed the mixture on the cardinal points of the devil's trap, the salt circle, and on the wall. She then stepped back to the altar and invoked the Horned God and the Goddess, calling on them to strengthen the spell.

Once again Avery floated off the ground, pulled upwards by an invisible force as energy raced through her like a lightning bolt. There was a crack in the air like thunder, and for a brief moment, the devil's trap and the protective semi-circle flashed with a dazzling bright white light, throwing them all out of the circle. They landed with a collective *thump* on the floor, and the candles went out, leaving them in complete darkness.

For a few seconds, there was only silence.

Avery was bone tired. The floor felt cold, hard, and dusty, and the energy that had raced through her body had gone, leaving her spent and exhausted.

Gil called out, "Is everyone okay?"

There was a general rumble of consent, and someone lit the candles, their warm glow once again illuminating the museum.

"I don't think I've ever channelled that much energy before," Briar said.

"I think I need to sleep for a week," Reuben added. He lay motionless, looking up at the ceiling. "I'm not used to that."

"You did well," El said, reaching over to pat his arm. "You're just out of practice."

"But it worked," Alex replied. She could hear the excitement in his voice. "That was amazing."

Avery rolled onto her side and looked over at him, grinning. "I know."

She heard footsteps and looked up to see Newton emerge from the shadows, his face grim in the half-light. She sat up. "Newton. I'd almost forgotten you were there. Are you okay?"

He stood looking over them. "I don't think I fully appreciated what you were before." His voice sounded flat and hard. "I didn't like it then, and I certainly don't like it now."

Disappointment coursed through Avery, but what did she expect? He wasn't a witch, whatever his background may be.

"Like it or not," Alex said, "we have protected that doorway. Now it doesn't matter what comes through. It won't get any further."

Newton glared down at them, his arms folded across his chest. "I will be keeping an eye on all of you, and for now, I'll be checking in every single day. And I expect one of you to come and check on this place *every single day*. Do you understand?"

Gil rose to his feet, belligerent. "Yes, we understand. But we're not the enemy, Newton."

"Well, until I know who the enemy is, you will remain firmly under my observation—unless, of course, you want to tell me exactly what is going on here?"

They remained silent, and he sneered. "No. I didn't think so. Well, I have a new job for you. You need to work out exactly how to get rid of that demon doorway so it's gone for good."

The group met at Alex's flat. By then it was nearly three in the morning and Avery was tired. The flat was warm and inviting after the chill of the museum, and they lounged around on the sofa or the floor, sipping beer or coffee. Avery had just told everyone about her encounter on the beach.

"So, who is this Faversham guy?" Alex asked. He lay on his side on the rug in front of the fireplace. "I already want to punch him."

Avery shrugged. "That's the trouble. I have no idea. He's not local—well, to White Haven anyway, and he's not in the written histories we have so far."

"Well, he seems to know a lot about us," Gil said, annoyed. "And Newton's pissed me off, too. We're not his bloody lackeys for him to be giving us stuff to do."

"Well, no," Reuben reasoned. He sat on the sofa, his legs stretched out in front of him. "But we want to get rid of the demon doorway, anyway."

"But how dare he tell us what to do! Like he controls us or something," Gil continued to complain.

"He was pretty mad," Briar agreed. "I'm not sure I'm comfortable with him knowing that much about us, but we don't have much choice."

"Wrong, Briar," Gil said, turning on her. "We could easily have broken into that place and done it without him."

"But we'd have risked being *more* implicated in the whole thing," El said. She was curled up in the corner of the sofa, sipping coffee. "I'm glad he was there. At least he knows we're trying to help, even if he was being a miserable git."

"What are we going to do about Faversham?" Alex asked. "At least in our homes and at work, he shouldn't be able to materialise out of thin air and attack us. But we're vulnerable anywhere else. We need to know more about him so we can defend ourselves."

"I'm going to go and visit that local author, if I can," Avery said. "He may have information he didn't share in his book."

"That's a good idea," Briar agreed, nodding. "I'd come with you, but I have to open up the shop all week."

"Me, too," El said, and most of the others agreed with her.

"That's okay. I'm happy to go alone."

"I'll come, if you can visit on Thursday. It's my day off," Alex explained. "I think from now on, we should probably work together."

Gil had been silent for a few minutes, but now he spoke. "This guy, Faversham, isn't a ghost. He's real. Have you looked him up?"

Avery suddenly felt incredibly stupid. "Er, no, actually. I was busy preparing spells. I didn't think."

Gil pulled his phone out of his back pocket. "Let's look now." It only took him a few minutes. "Thank the gods for Google. Caspian Faversham, head of finance at Kernow Industries in Harecombe." Harecombe was the next town down along the coast. He turned the phone around and showed Avery a photo. "This him?"

She reached for the phone and had a closer look. His smug, handsome face was looking back at her, all smiles in his sharp suit. "That's him!" She passed the phone around so the others got a look at him.

Gil grinned. "Well, at least we know who he is now. Our enemy number one."

"I've heard of that company," Briar said.

"Everyone's heard of them, surely," Alex said, handing the phone back to Gil. "They're huge."

"And," Gil added, after looking at his phone again, "his father is the head of the company. Mr Sebastian Faversham. And what a silver-haired fox he is," he said snarkily, showing them his photo, too.

"So," El said, "he doesn't mind us knowing who he is, or he'd have never told you his name. He'd have known you'd look him up."

"Eventually," Gil said, teasing Avery.

"Oh, sod off, Gil. I was busy," Avery said, fearing she'd never live this down. "So he's a powerful witch—or sorcerer. Do you think silver fox Faversham is a witch, too?"

"Probably," El said. "Feels like a declaration of war to me. Sort of—*this is who we are, and there's nothing you can do about it.* They have money and power. And he must be the one who placed the doorway on the wall."

"So he's a murderer, too," Reuben said.

"But we have what they want," Alex put in, grinning from his spot on the rug.

Avery nodded. "I presume then that you two," she said, looking at El and Alex, "are not prepared to give up your grimoires?"

"No!" they both replied.

"Good. Not sure how he'll take that news, though."

Eighteen

A very spent the week working hard, both in the shop and reading Anne's work. Faversham hadn't reappeared, and there were no further deaths. Although their trap hadn't captured any demons, at least none had been unleashed on the unsuspecting community, either.

She had managed to contact Samuel Kingston, the local author, and had arranged to meet him with Alex. It was Thursday morning, and outside it was cloudy and threatened rain. They sat in Avery's battered van in front of an unassuming cottage on the edge of White Haven.

"Well, it looks safe enough," Alex decided, peering at it.

"He's a historian; what did you expect?"

He shrugged and turned back to her. "Maybe I'm paranoid, but I'm expecting a lot of weird things at the moment."

She looked at him properly for the first time after picking him up on the corner outside the pub. "You look tired. What have you been up to?"

"Oh, cheers." He flipped down the passenger sunscreen and looked at his reflection in the mirror. "I do a bit, don't I?" He ran his hands through his hair and gave her a rakish grin. "I've been experimenting with my grimoire. It was four in the morning before I got to sleep today."

"I hope you're not doing anything too dangerous," she said, starting to feel a bit worried.

"Just stretching my powers a bit."

"Like what?"

"Honing my psychic skills, spirit-walking, practising banishing spells." He paused, looking at her with raised eyebrows.

"All right, I'll bite. Banishing spells?"

"For getting rid of unwanted spirits and demons and other creatures that may cross dimensions they shouldn't." He leaned back, looking pleased with himself.

Avery had to admit she was impressed. And infuriatingly, his dishevelled, smug face looked just as handsome as he normally did—not that she wanted him to know that. "Great! So hopefully you'll be of some use now!" she said cheekily, and hopped out of the car before he could respond.

He leapt out of the passenger side. "You're not that funny, you know that?"

She grinned and headed up to the house. "Come on. Kingston will wonder what we're doing out here."

The cottage, like many in the area, was old with a thatched roof. The windows were small, and there was a pretty garden running riot with summer plants on either side of the garden path.

They knocked, and a middle-aged woman opened the door. She was dressed in a smart blue skirt and blouse, and she smiled at them immediately. "You must be Samuel's guests?"

Avery smiled back at her. "Yes, I'm Avery, and this is Alex."

She stepped aside. "Come on in. I'm his daughter, Alice. I'll take you through. He's so excited to have visitors and to be able to talk about his book. I hope you're ready—he may just talk you to death."

She shut the door and led them down the long hall to the back of the house. "I'm heading out to work, so I'll leave you to it."

She led them past old photos and watercolours of the local area. The cottage had been modernised. The floors were stripped back to beautiful wood that shone with a high gloss varnish, and the walls were painted muted pastels. She led them into a conservatory at the back of the house, filled with greenery and looking over the back garden that was as packed with plants as the front.

"Dad," she called, "they're here."

She turned to them. "You may have to speak up. His hearing's not as good as it used to be."

An elderly man turned to them from a large cane chair that sat in front of a long window. His shoulders were bowed, his hair shot through with grey, and he had glasses perched on the end of his nose. He squinted up at them, and Avery smiled. As he saw his guests, he tried to rise to his feet with a beaming smile.

"Hi, Mr Kingston. I'm Avery—I spoke to you on the phone about your book. I've brought my friend along, Alex, if that's okay?"

"Of course, of course," he said, reaching forward and shaking their outstretched hands. Avery immediately liked him. He seemed so sweet and was so pleased to see them. He looked beyond them to his daughter. "Can you bring us a pot of tea, dear, before you go?"

She nodded. "Give me two minutes."

Samuel ushered them into seats; a small table sat between them, filled with papers and a plate of biscuits.

He smiled at them again. "I don't often have visitors wanting to talk about my book. This is a real treat."

"It's treat for us too, Mr Kingston," Avery said. "I was so impressed with your research."

"Call me Sam," he insisted. "It took me years, my dear, but I love White Haven. I've lived here all my life. It's my tribute to the place."

Alex leaned forward. "I confess I haven't read it yet, Sam, but I will."

He waved his hand as if brushing something away. "That's fine. You're young, you have time."

Before Alex could answer, Samuel's daughter came in with a tray containing a pot of tea, cups, sugar, and milk, and placed it on the table. "Right, I'm off," she said to him. "Got everything you need?"

"I'm fine. Stop worrying," he said to her.

She smiled at Alex and Avery over his head. "Have fun, then." And she left them to it.

After a few minutes of small talk, and settling them all in with tea and biscuits, Samuel started to tell them how he came to write the book. He asked, "Is there anything in particular you were interested in? I cover a lot of history."

"I'm interested in the witch trials," Avery said, placing her cup on the table and taking a biscuit. "I was wondering where you got some of the information from, and if there was anything you left out?"

He looked at her speculatively, his mind lively despite his physical frailty. "Left out? Why do you ask that?"

She glanced at Alex. "I'm aware there are certain old families that have lived in White Haven for generations, and you mention several of them in your book. Obviously there's Helena Marchmont who was burned as a result of the witch trials, and some others who were drowned. You mention the names of those who were investigated, such as the Bonnevilles and Jacksons, but I wonder if there are some you didn't mention? Some families that may still be around today."

He nodded slowly and sighed. "The witch trials were dark times, very dark. A time of madness, it seems to me. Neighbours turned on neighbours, you know. Old friends betrayed each other, while others tried to protect each other." He paused for a moment, thinking. "I wanted to say more, but my publishers wanted me to stick to the facts. They said I would be speculating, and we might upset any descendants who still lived in the area. They didn't want to risk being sued. I can see their point, but I knew I was right."

"Right about what?"

"I think Helena was betrayed."

Avery couldn't have been more shocked if he had reached across the table and slapped her. A quick glance at Alex showed he was as surprised as she was.

"What do you mean, *betrayed*?" Her biscuit lay forgotten in her lap.

Samuel took a deep breath in and looked out at the garden, his eyes narrowed in thought. Avery's heart was beating fast, and she tried to calm herself down. The old man might be getting excited over nothing.

He eventually spoke. "In the archives, you can see the old names, the ones who had money and stature in the village, mentioned time and time again. You've mentioned some, the Bonnevilles and Jacksons, but there were also the Ashworths and Kershaws." Avery recognised Elspeth's and Briar's family names. Samuel continued, "These families would have known each other, were probably friends. It's hard to say, of course," he hedged, spreading his hands and shrugging. "But they were of equal standing in the community, so it makes sense. But there were other families mentioned who were equally well known. One family were ship owners, wealthy, who lived outside of White Haven, but had a big presence in it. They employed people in their shipping industry. I mention them because they testified against Helena Marchmont, and I believe, because of their standing in the town, heavily influenced the trial against her—despite protestations of innocence from the other families I've mentioned."

"Who were they?" Avery asked, fearing she already knew the answer.

"The Favershams. Because of them, I had to leave their name out of the book."

Avery felt a cold shudder run through her, and she looked at Alex, trying to gather her wits.

"I'm confused. How did they know you were going to put them in your book in the first place?" Alex asked. He leaned forward, his elbows on his knees, looking at Samuel intently.

Samuel shrugged. "I interviewed them. It's part of the process. They're well known, and when I saw their name I thought it would be good to get a present day perspective on the whole thing, thinking it would be a bit light-hearted. I had no idea they would take against the idea so strongly." He thought for a moment. "It got very ugly, very quickly. Before I'd even got home they'd phoned my publisher, and that was that. I was going to look at other local interviews, but that got quashed, too."

"Did they give a reason?"

"No, not really. Other than that it would damage their reputation." He gave a short bark of a laugh. "It's over 500 years ago! Who cares, really?" Samuel looked at them, perplexed. "It was their reaction that actually made me more suspicious. Do you know that since then those archives have been locked?"

"Locked!" Avery finally found her voice again.

He nodded. "Most of the records are kept at the Courtney Library in Truro. That's where I got a lot of my information. Now, that particular archive is locked." He smiled sadly. "Money can buy you a lot."

Avery took a deep breath. "Wow. That's fascinating. Thank you, Samuel. You didn't have to share that."

"My dear, I'm getting older, and who else can I share it with? No one else can see those records now, and I doubt anyone cares to." He leaned forward, a twinkle in his eye. "Why are you asking?"

The last thing she wanted to do was endanger the old man, but he'd been honest, so she felt she should be too. "I'm related to Helena Marchmont, and I've become interested recently in what really happened back then."

His eyes widened with surprise. "Ah! I should have realised." He tapped his head. "I'm slower than I used to be. Of course, you're from Happenstance Books."

She nodded. "And Alex is a Bonneville."

He looked at Alex, who shrugged. "I guess we've both got the history bug lately."

"Well," Samuel said, "I wish you luck on your research, but I'm not sure you'll get very far."

"Have you got any copies of the old archives?"

Samuel shook his head. "No, unfortunately not. It was all in my old notes, and I regret to say I haven't got them anymore. I just didn't have the room when I moved here. I burnt the lot of them." He fell silent for a moment, and then said, "I never used to believe in witchcraft, despite the fact that I've lived here for years. It's a magical place, and the town thrives on the history, but I always thought it was all a bit of fun. But after meeting the Favershams, I became a believer. Be careful around them. They're dangerous."

Nineteen

A very was sitting at a table in a beer garden overlooking the sea and Alex sat opposite, each with a pint of the local beer called Doom in front of them. It was another hot day, just before the lunchtime rush, and they had secured a table under a broad umbrella that gave them some welcome shade.

"I think we need to go to the Courtney Library," Alex said, looking out at the sea thoughtfully.

"Now?" Avery asked, surprised. "What's the point? We can't see anything."

He turned to her and grinned. "We can see what it looks like, where the archives are, and check that the restrictions haven't changed. And then, if we need to, we can break in at night."

She nearly choked on her pint. "Are you insane? What do you mean, 'break in?'"

"We want to see those archives, right?"

"I'm not sure we need to. We already know who the Favershams are and that they testified against Helena. I'm not sure any more details will help." She took a sip of her beer. "What we need to do is work out how to protect ourselves against Faversham."

"But the more we know," Alex argued, "the better prepared we'd be. There might be a useful nugget of information about the trials that could unlock everything for us."

"And we might get arrested and learn nothing."

"We're witches, Ave. Stop thinking so laterally. We can spell ourselves into shadows, disarm alarm systems, and sneak in." He tapped his head. "Think!"

"Alex! I don't do magic to get sneaky stuff done."

"We don't normally fight demons and make devil's traps, either. Times change."

They were interrupted by the arrival of the waitress with their lunch. Avery had opted for seafood chowder, and Alex had steak and chips. Once she'd gone, Alex continued.

"We have to be the aggressor here, or we'll be trampled on. We need to up our game. I don't like being on the back foot." He took a large mouthful of steak.

Avery's stomach grumbled and she took a sip of the chowder as she thought about Alex's proposition. "I guess it won't hurt to look. And I suppose that also explains why there's no mention of Faversham in Anne's stuff."

Alex nodded and pointed with his fork. "Correct. And there may be more old families Samuel didn't think to mention, including the Newtons. I'd rather look myself and know for certain."

"I wonder if our Newton knew about this?"

"Maybe not. If we know so very little of our own history, why would he?"

As Avery looked up, she saw a man approaching them from across the beer garden and her throat tightened. "*Alex*. Caspian Faversham is here, and he's heading this way."

"*What*?"

Alex spun around on his seat, simultaneously pushing his plate away. They both stood as Caspian made his way through the tables and arrived next to them. He looked at Alex, assessing him. They were matched in height, but Alex was broader in build. Caspian was dressed in a shirt and smart jeans and looked like he was about to visit a country club; Alex was dressed in an old t-shirt and faded jeans, and his long hair was loose. They were like chalk and cheese.

Caspian gave a thin-lipped smile and acknowledged Avery with a dismissive glance. "Mr Bonneville. Why don't we sit?" he said in his irritating, condescending tone.

"Because I don't want to," Alex said. "Who the hell do you think you are?"

"Now, now," Caspian began, looking around as heads turned towards them. "Let's not cause a scene."

He sat on the bench next to Avery so he could face Alex, and Avery edged to the far end of the bench to get some distance between them.

Alex grimaced, but finally sat down. "I know what you want, and the answer is no," he said, cutting through the niceties.

"I see. Have you thought through the consequences?" Caspian watched him, his hands resting together on the table.

"Whatever the consequences are, it's still no."

"So, you don't care that your friends, or you, may die when I come to take your grimoire?"

"What makes you think you're stronger than us?" Alex asked, his eyes hard.

"I know I am. I have been practising my magic for years. You have simply *played* with yours."

Alex smiled. "Sticks and stones, Caspian. Those grimoires are ours, left to us by our families. You have no right to them. Besides, if your magic is so superior, what do you need our grimoires for?"

"Let's just say we are owed them, but were cheated out of them many years ago."

"Bullshit," Alex said. He paused, watching Caspian's face. "You know what? I think all this talk about the Witchfinder General is a cover for why the grimoires were really hidden. Our ancestors were hiding them from your family, and you've been waiting and watching. Well, you can keep on waiting. We're on to you, Faversham. Now piss off, and go tell your daddy there's no deal."

Caspian jerked back as if he'd been slapped. "Your family has always been stupid." He turned to Avery, "As has yours. You have no idea what you're messing with."

Avery once again felt the wind whip around her. "Maybe not, Caspian, but we'll find out. And when we do, *we'll* come looking for *you*."

Caspian stood up and looked at them both with disdain, but also with something else. *Was there a flash of fear in his expression?* "Another time, then," he said, before he turned his back and left them.

Avery took a deep breath and exhaled slowly. "I'd love to know how he keeps finding us."

"Probably a simple finding spell," Alex guessed. He grinned. "I think we successfully pissed him off. Although, he has interrupted a perfectly good lunch."

"What made you say that the Witchfinder General is a cover?" Avery asked, remembering what he'd said to Caspian. "We've never discussed that before."

"Just a feeling I have. It popped into my mind while I was looking at his smug, arrogant face. I'm right, though—I'd put money on it."

An idea started to form in Avery's mind, but before she could say anything else, Alex's phone rang, and he pulled it out of his pocket.

"It's Gil," he said, and quickly answered it, leaving Avery worried something else may have happened while they'd been away. "Hey Gil," he said, "what's up?" Avery watched him as he nodded, and grunted,

"Yes, no, really?" He looked at Avery, eyebrows raised. "Yep, we'll head back now." He put his phone down and said, "Eat up. They think they know where his grimoire may be. They want our help. And we need to change clothing."

Avery paused, a chunk of bread halfway to her mouth. "Are you kidding?"

"Nope." He winked. "We'll put off our visit to the archives for another time."

Avery and Alex turned off the road and onto a long drive that wound through tall trees and dense bushes, until the drive ended in a broad sweep in front of a sprawling manor house. It had originally been built in the 14th century, but had been added to over the years so it featured a variety of styles. Avery loved it. It was old and welcoming, made of mellow stone with mullioned windows.

The grounds were extensive; a mixture of lawns, gardens, and woodland, and the garden directly behind the house descended in a series of terraces down to the sea, where they ended at a steep cliff. A large section of grounds at the front of the house were accessed by a different driveway, and housed Gil's plant nurseries that were open to the public.

Avery parked at the side of the drive and they headed around the back of the house and down to the glasshouse where Gil and Reuben were waiting for them. El was there as well, but there was no sign of Briar. All three of them were dressed in boots, jeans, and hooded tops. They carried backpacks, lanterns, and torches.

The glasshouse behind them was huge. It had a brick base with high, arched windows and a glass roof housed in cast iron above it. It was beautiful.

"What's going on?" Avery asked.

"We're heading into the tunnel beneath the glasshouse, that's what's going on," Gil said, running his hand though his hair.

"There's a tunnel beneath the greenhouse?" Alex asked, squinting at it.

"Glasshouse," Gil corrected. "And yes, a smuggling tunnel. Our family has a dubious history, and access to the beach."

"You'd always known about the tunnel?" Alex asked.

Reuben answered, "We knew about the cellars and the tunnel that ran to the ice house, and we think there's a tunnel that runs to Old Haven Church, but we didn't know about *this* tunnel!"

Avery started to feel excited. "Why? Where does it go?"

"Over there," Gil said, pointing to the small island that sat off the coast.

"Are you serious?" Images of dark, dank passages filled her brain. And of course there was the risk of drowning, which at this point overshadowed the fear of attack by demons.

"And how did you find it?" Alex asked, equally amazed by the look on his face.

"It's a long story involving family archives, Anne's notes, and our existing grimoire. And luck. We found the entrance just before we phoned you, but thought the more the merrier."

"Probably a good idea," Alex said, and he described their latest encounter with Caspian. "We need to look into something that can protect us from his unexpected visits—something that will block us from his search spells."

"I've been thinking about that," Reuben said. "I have an idea, if you're open to having a tattoo."

Alex shrugged. "I like ink. But why?"

"I'm working on a design for a tattoo that will protect us from prying eyes—including demons. I think we should try it."

"Well, I've never had a tattoo, but I'll try anything to keep Faversham away," Avery said, thinking that it was great that Reuben was getting more involved. "So, what's going on with you and magic, Reuben? Are you in, or out?"

He shrugged. "It complicates my life, and I don't like complicated. I like ink, the wind, and the surf. But I also don't like being attacked. So, for now, I'm in."

Avery nodded. "Fair enough."

"What's the plan this afternoon?" Alex asked.

"We've found the entrance, we're pretty sure we know where it goes, so we're going to check it out. And that's the plan," Gil explained.

"Simple. I like it. It's vague on the finer points, but hell, we were planning to break into some archives before you phoned."

El looked at them both. "Okay, sounds like you have more to catch us up on. In the meantime, let's head to the tunnels. Briar can't make it, and I've bunked off work. Let's go."

They followed Gil into the glasshouse. Long benches ran along both sides and down the centre. Tender plants jostled with seedlings and tomato plants, and the smell was rich and pungent. Gil led them down to the far end where there was a hatch in the ground, and he headed down into the darkness, his torch flickering to life.

"Why is there a tunnel under here?" Avery asked, feeling more and more baffled. She pulled her torch free as she spoke, preparing to follow the others.

El jumped in to explain. "It seems there's a heating system for the glasshouse, from way back. Pipes, a furnace, water. Very sophisticated. There would have been an outside entrance at some point, but it was bricked up and the chimney removed. And there's a hidden doorway. Well—not hidden anymore!"

At the bottom of the steps there was a room stretching the length of the glasshouse. It had a brick-lined floor and a low ceiling, the cast iron pipes clearly visible above them.

Gil spoke from the shadows. "This glasshouse fell into disrepair before World War I. The structure completely collapsed, and it was overgrown. It wasn't until the Second World War that it was repaired—you know, to support the war effort. I think that's why my crazy uncle never found it. We came down here as a last resort, really."

"I'd almost forgotten about him," Avery said. "How does he tie in with the Favershams?"

"No idea. He may not be linked at all."

Gil turned and led the way to the wall where an old furnace sat. To its left was a long row of shelves, now deconstructed and stacked on the floor. Wooden panels lined the wall behind the shelves with numerous hooks attached, but within the panels a door-shaped black space loomed.

"Voila!" Gil exclaimed, looking pleased.

Alex laughed. "Wow. How did you find that?"

"By a systematic poking and prodding of panels and pulling of hooks."

"Yeah, right," Reuben said, his voice dripping with sarcasm. "It was *so* random."

"Cheers, Reu," Gil murmured. "And now, onward we go."

Gil set off with an enthusiastic march, and the others followed him into the passage beyond. Avery shivered. It was cold, damp, and musty, and she wrapped her hoodie more firmly around her as they headed further along the passage.

Their torches illuminated the brick floor and walls, which curved in an arch overhead, but as they went deeper the tunnel changed into bare earth and rock, the surfaces rough and unfinished. Water dripped from overhead, and the air smelt stale.

"It must have been years since anyone walked down here," Avery mused, carefully watching her step.

"Probably close to a hundred at least," Reuben called back.

The ground sloped downwards, following the gradient of the hill towards the shore, and then it quickly got steeper, with rudimentary steps carved out of the earth. Every now and again they passed brackets for torches on the walls, but the torches were long gone. Eventually they emerged into a larger space, where the remnants of broken and rotting crates were on the ground.

"Are we all okay to carry on?" Gil asked.

"May as well," Alex said. He looked around with interest. "Is this a smuggling cave?"

"Maybe. This could be where they stored some stuff."

Alex laughed. "Well, I wouldn't have taken your family for smugglers, Gil, but I guess you had to get your money from somewhere!"

"Sod off!" Gil said, annoyed. "We were doing people a favour."

"I'm kidding!" Alex said, rolling his eyes. "You know, you were probably stealing from the Favershams, and anything that upsets them is fine with me. I don't know them and I hate them."

"Why the Favershams?" Gil called back.

"Because they were a trading company."

"Good, I hope we really annoyed them," Reuben put in.

They pressed on, and the passage became wider and higher. Every so often a small clump of earth appeared on the ground as if there'd been a slip, but in general the passage looked in good condition.

"How long does this go on for?" El asked.

"Until we get to the island, I guess," Reuben said. "It's half a mile off shore."

They were now a long way from the entrance, and deep underground. Water streamed down the wall in places and it was muddy underfoot. The passageway started to rise again, and then opened out, and they stumbled into a large cave.

The group let out a collective sigh of wonder. The cave was full of wooden crates.

"Excellent! This could be it!" Gil said, as he headed to the nearest crate and lit his lantern.

"It's going to take ages," Reuben grumbled. He flashed his torch around and up, revealing a high, rocky ceiling. "I think we must be under the island now, so there has to be an exit here somewhere. In fact," he stood and listened for a moment, "I can hear the sea."

He was right. Avery could also hear the soft shush of the waves, and the occasional louder crash as waves hit rocks. "I'll help you find the entrance, Reu, while the others search the crates."

"Sure," he nodded, and they headed off to the far side of the cave, leaving the others to discuss spells to help reveal the crate.

"What if it's not here?" Avery asked Reuben, as she played her torch along the cave wall.

He shrugged. "We keep on searching."

Avery caught sight of sand on the ground and headed towards it. "Reuben, it must be over here." She saw an exit behind a jutting wall of rock leading into another passageway, a light trail of sand snaking down the centre. Avery grinned. "Shall we?"

"After you," he said.

The further they travelled, the thicker the sand became, and the louder the sound of the surf. And then they came to a dead end.

"It must be a hidden door," Reuben said. "After all, you don't want everyone finding a smuggler's cave."

"I guess not. Do you think it's sealed with magic?"

"I doubt it. Not all smugglers would have been witches."

They started to feel around the wall and the floor, looking for a hidden catch or mechanism, until Reuben shouted, "Got it."

He had reached his hand into a natural crack in the rock about halfway down the wall. Avery heard a *click*, and the wall in front of them opened a fraction down the right side. She pushed it open cautiously, but it was stiff from lack of use, and she pushed against it with her shoulders until it creaked open.

Beyond the door was a pale light and Avery stepped onto soft sand, Reuben close behind her. They were in another cave. This one was long with a low roof and the ground was covered with soft white sand; up ahead was a slight break in the rock where a pale light filtered in.

They made their way cautiously to the gap and peered through into another cave that opened up to the sea. It was empty, and there was no one in sight. The entrance to the cave was covered in brambles, bushes, and stunted trees, but beyond the greenery they could see the blue-grey sparkle of water.

"We're on the far side of Gull Island," Reuben said. "If I remember correctly, there's a huge hill of rock above us. It would hide any ships docked out there."

They peered through the branches onto the shore beyond. It was a mix of rock and sand, and sharper rocks broke through the surface of the sea. "They'd have to bring a small boat through those. It would be tricky to navigate," Reuben observed.

Avery turned towards the back of the cave. From where she stood, the narrow entrance to the cave beyond was completely hidden by the curve of the rock wall. She nodded. "Very cool. I wonder if anyone else knows about this place?"

"Not anymore, I'd imagine," Reuben mused, shaking his head. "From the sea, you wouldn't be able to see this cave." He slipped through the tangle of branches until he could stand on the shore, and he looked up. "It's so steep above us, no one could clamber down. Not unless they had climbing equipment."

Avery joined him, trying to not get scratched, and looking up realised he was right. "They chose this place well. I wonder how they ever discovered it?"

"I guess we'll never know." Reuben looked at the sea and the small cove. "I bet this place would be pretty inaccessible on stormy nights."

For a few seconds, Avery tried to imagine what it would have been like centuries before, with ships anchoring off the coast and trying to bring their goods ashore under the cover of darkness. She shivered. A lot of people died smuggling, and she doubted it would have been any different here.

"It must be weird, knowing your ancestors were smugglers."

"It's even weirder knowing they're witches," he said, laughing.

They sat on the shore, enjoying the warmth of the sun on their faces, and Avery turned to look at Reuben's strong profile. "You wish you were surfing, don't you?" she said, smiling.

"Not there I don't," he countered, looking at the rocks.

It wasn't often that Avery was alone with Reuben, so while she had the chance she asked, "Why don't you use your magic?"

He dropped his gaze to the ground and then looked at her, his expression honest. "It feels like cheating, I suppose. When I'm surfing, it feels like it's just me and the sea, and if I used my magic it would make it too easy. I stopped using it in my teens, and haven't really used it since. Until now, of course. The spell the other night to cast the devil's trap was harder than I thought. I've been knackered for days."

"Have you been practising?"

"Yeah, just learning how to control it, really. I forgot how natural it felt. It's coming back, though, quicker than I thought. I've been practising on the grounds and in the attic when Alicia's not around."

"Do you think she knows? I mean, about you two? It seems mad to me that you could be with someone that long and not know," Avery said, finally expressing her doubts about Alicia's ignorance of their magic.

Reuben looked thoughtful for a few seconds. "I don't think she does, but sometimes I wonder."

"Why?" Avery pressed, unsure as to why it should even matter.

"It's like she wilfully turns away if Gil even starts to talk about things that aren't everyday-normal, like she doesn't want to encourage the discussion."

"Maybe she's uncomfortable with it, and would rather pretend it doesn't exist," Avery reasoned. She could understand that. She'd like to do the same with demons.

Reuben added, "But he's been spending a lot of time with you guys recently, and she hasn't batted an eye. And if I'm honest, I think that's weird. I mean, I'd be asking questions, but she doesn't."

Avery looked back over the sea and had a very unpleasant idea. All this time, she'd been wondering about how Caspian Faversham could know what they were up to. Someone had to have told him about Anne and their research. *Could it be Alicia?* She knew Gil had told her a heavily censored version of their activities, but maybe she knew more than she was letting on. She exhaled heavily and chastised herself. It was a ridiculous idea.

"Why do you ask?" Reuben said, looking puzzled.

"Oh, no reason. Just curious, I guess," she said offhandedly. The last thing she wanted to do was cause problems with pointless suspicions; maybe she should ask Alex. She decided to change the subject. "Well, I guess we should turn back. At least we know there's nothing else hidden here. The others will think we've got lost."

She stood up and dusted sand off her legs, and then led the way back through the caves to the hidden doorway, both of them dragging a bundle of gorse in an attempt to disguise their footprints, just in case. Once through the exit, they sealed it off behind them, making their way back to the others. Within minutes they heard screams and shouts.

"Crap! What now?" Avery said, hoping it wasn't more demons, as she broke into a run.

Twenty

A very skidded to a halt at the entrance to the cave, smacking into the back of Reuben, who ran far quicker than her. She pushed him out of the way, wondering what he had stopped for.

The cave was dimly lit with light from the lanterns they'd carried with them. Faversham stood in the centre of the room, a vast creature rearing up next to him, made out of what appeared to be sand and stone. It seemed to have short, stubby legs, but long arms, and it swept them outwards, trying to grab Alex and El, who dodged out of its grasp whilst sending blasts of energy at it. She couldn't see Gil at all.

"What the hell is *that*?" Reuben exclaimed.

Avery didn't answer. She didn't care what it was, but she presumed it was somehow being controlled by Faversham, and he hadn't seen them yet. The sight of him looking smug was enough to infuriate her. *How the hell did he keep finding them so quickly?*

Avery summoned her powers and sent a blast of air towards him at a blistering pace, like a tornado. The noise of the lumbering beast was so loud that Faversham couldn't hear it coming, and he looked around too late. It smashed into him, carrying him into the far wall with a resounding *smack*. He fell to the ground, dazed, and the creature started to lose cohesion as it slowed to a stop.

Avery didn't hesitate. She loosed another wave of air and energy straight at the rock monster, and it staggered, turning towards her with a roar.

Instinctively, she drew on the air again and it lifted her clean off her feet until she floated over the ground. Without having any idea what she was trying to do, she rushed forwards, aiming a blast of pure energy from her hands towards the centre of its mass. The creature came to a stuttering halt.

In the lull from the attack, Avery saw Alex and El release a stream of fire at Faversham, who was trying to rise to his feet. He looked furious, but their attack caught him off guard and he scrambled for cover.

Avery renewed her attack on the beast, enveloping it in another tornado, until, with a deafening roar, it broke apart, sending sand and rock blasting in all directions. A large chunk of stone caught her in the gut and threw her backwards onto the pile of crates, the impact making her dazed and nauseous.

Despite the hit, she couldn't stop. Not now. She staggered to her feet, wobbling on the boxes beneath her.

Avery saw Alex and El standing shoulder to shoulder below her. Faversham was back on his feet, sending a jet of sand and earth at them. They struggled under the onslaught, throwing up a shield in front of them. Avery directed her magic at one of the crates and picked it up with a whoosh of air, hurling it over Alex and El. At the last second Faversham looked up, but it was too late and the crate smacked into him, crushing him beneath its weight.

Once again, Alex and El combined their powers and sent a stream of fire at Faversham's dazed and broken body. Although she couldn't reach them, Avery added her magic to theirs, enhancing their fire with air, until it turned white-hot. Unable to tolerate their combined attack, Faversham disappeared.

Avery collapsed on the crates, vaguely wondering what had happened to Gil and Reuben. And then she heard Reuben's frantic shouts coming from somewhere below her. "Gil, Gil, wake up!"

Avery sat up, and her adrenalin kicked in. Gil must have been injured. She slid towards the sound of Reuben's voice, the crates wobbling and sliding beneath her, and then she saw them. Gil was lying at the rear of the cave, covered in blood, and Reuben was cradling him in his arms. Gil was horribly still.

She half lurched and half ran towards them, until she fell on her knees next to them both, Alex and El arriving at the same time. Reuben was sobbing, almost breathless as he hugged Gil.

Alex leaned in close, feeling for a pulse, but Gil had a huge head injury, she could tell from here, and his head fell at the wrong angle. A wild panic surged through Avery. Gil looked dead. It couldn't be true. She wouldn't believe it.

"I can run back and call an ambulance," she said, feeling her voice breaking, as she desperately tried to remain calm and rational.

El was silent next to her, in complete shock, and Reuben was inconsolable.

Alex looked at Avery. "I don't think we can save him, Ave. I think his neck's broken."

Avery started to shake all over, as tears overtook her, and she sat back, letting grief flow over her. Alex was right.

"El," Alex called softly. "Can you—" he gestured towards Reuben, and El nodded, her face white as she eased her way to Reuben and put her arms around him, while he cradled Gill in his lap.

Alex crawled next to Avery and put his arms around her, pulling her close, and she returned his hug, wrapping her arms around him and burying her face in his chest.

For a few minutes, there was only silence. Avery felt as if she had fallen into a black hole, and the only thing that stopped her from slipping away completely was Alex. His solid warmth was the most comforting thing she could hope for, and she felt his head rest on hers as he pulled her even closer. His body trembled and she looked up at him, smoothing his hair away from his face. His cheeks were wet.

"What happened?"

He shook his head. "I don't know. I have no idea where that bastard came from." He paused for a second, thinking. "We were searching the crates and trying spells, and all of a sudden, Faversham was there, and he blasted us right off our feet. Then that creature appeared. The thing is, I don't think he expected us to be so strong. He demanded that we back off and we refused, and it all went mad after that. Gil was caught by that thing and got thrown against the rock. I didn't even see you arrive. I think he would have killed all of us if you hadn't come."

Reuben spoke then, his voice ragged. "I'm going to kill that bastard. He started a war he will *not* win. And all for a damn book."

Avery pulled free from Alex. "Did you find it?"

Alex shook his head. "No. Not a trace."

"Did Faversham know?" Avery couldn't believe that Gil was dead, and they hadn't even found the book.

"I don't think so. He didn't ask questions."

"We need to get out of here. Faversham could come back at any moment. And we need to call the police. We have to report Gil's death."

"What the hell are we going to say?" El asked, finally speaking.

"We tell them we came searching the caves, and Gil fell from the top of the crates. We keep Faversham's name out of it—no one will believe in witchcraft, and we can't reveal ourselves."

"And what about Newton?" El asked.

"We'll deal with Newton when the time comes. You stay here with Reuben, and we'll come back with help. Reuben," Avery asked gently, "are you okay to stay here with El?"

Reuben nodded. "Whatever. I'm not leaving Gil."

"No, of course not. I'll go with Alex, and El can wait with you." She looked at El, who nodded her agreement.

"And you better find Alicia, too," Reuben added.

Avery felt her heart sink even more. *How would she take it?*

"Of course."

Alex rose to his feet and extending his hand, pulled Avery up next to him. He looked at El and Reuben. "I'm worried about leaving you. Faversham might come back."

El reassured him. "He won't come back. He looked injured to me. I think we broke his arm. And he must have used a lot of energy to control whatever that thing was."

"Come on, let's go," Avery said, and they headed to the passage that would lead them back to the glasshouse.

For a while they walked in silence, Avery wondering how to broach the subject of Alicia, but Alex spoke first.

"Are you all right?"

She tried to hold back tears. "Not really, but we have to get through this first."

He nodded and a guilty look flashed across his face. "I'm wondering if there's some sort of spell we can use for Gil."

She looked at him sharply. "No way. You don't mess with that stuff. People die, Alex."

"I know, but Gil's been murdered! He's gone. He's our friend!" Alex was almost shouting, a pleading look in his eyes.

They came to an awkward stop, their voices resounding in the enclosed space.

"Of course he's our friend, but he's dead, and we *cannot* bring him back." Her voice broke into a sob. "We're not monsters, Alex."

Alex hugged her close again, wrapping his arms around her. Avery cried properly now. Big, long sobs wracked her body as she felt the shock washing through her, and she felt him shaking, too. Alex felt so strong and so warm that she wanted to stay there forever. But now was not the time. She pulled back. "I'm sorry."

"Don't apologise. I shouldn't have asked. It was stupid, and you're right. But I feel guilty. Gil didn't really want to do this. I'm afraid it's my fault he's dead."

Avery shook her head. "We can't do this. Not here. Not now. We underestimated Faversham—we won't again. Come on. We need to get moving."

"But where's the book? It has to be here somewhere. We can't have gone through all this for nothing."

A sudden thought struck Avery, and she smacked her head with her palm. "We've been so stupid! How can we have thought the book would have been in pile of crates used by smugglers as recently as the last two hundred years? They would have found something."

"Shit." Alex closed his eyes for a second. "We need to get smarter about this."

"Come on. We'll think as we walk."

Alex released his hold and the cold air swirled around Avery again as they continued up the passage.

"What do you know about Alicia?" Avery asked, deciding she had to bring this up.

"Not much, why?"

"Because someone's betraying us. There's no way Faversham could know where we were today."

"He must be using a finding spell!"

"But he knows too much!"

"And you think it's Alicia? That's a big accusation."

"I know, and I don't say this lightly, but think, Alex! How else could he know what's going on?"

"But how does Alicia know? She doesn't even know Gil's a witch!"

"We don't know that. He could have been deceived by her for years." Avery stopped again and told him about her conversation with Reuben. "All of this started when I received the note from Anne. *Faversham mentioned Anne.* He knew her name! How could he possibly know that?"

Alex rubbed his hands across his face, and the torchlight flickered wildly along the walls. "I suppose that makes sense." He sounded tired and despondent. "So, what do we do? Do we pretend we don't know?"

"I think we play it by ear. It depends what she does now. Gil's dead, and it will be interesting to see how she deals with that." She paused. "Sorry, that sounded really cold, but you know what I mean."

Alex nodded. "I know. Are we going to tell the others?"

"I think we have to. Do you trust the others?"

"Reuben, Briar, and El? Yes! Absolutely."

Avery took a deep breath and exhaled slowly. "Good. Me, too."

"Come on," Alex said. "Time to call the police."

Twenty-One

A very woke up at three in the morning in a tangle of sheets in Alex's bed. He was sleeping on the sofa, and she wasn't sure if she was pleased at his gentlemanly behaviour or incredibly disappointed.

She had woken from a deep sleep with a racing mind and lots of questions. And then she thought of Gil, and tears started to well again. Gil was dead. She still couldn't believe it. She rolled over and stretched out, going through the events of the previous day.

It had been a horrible few hours. The police had arrived, and finally Gil's body had been removed from the cave. Reuben and Elspeth had emerged white and shaken, and all of them had been interviewed on site by the police. DI Newton had interrogated them all with barely concealed hostility, and said they were to remain at home and that he would see them all the next day. However, their story had been believed—at least by most people.

Despite trying to call Alicia several times, they couldn't reach her, and had instead passed it on to the police. Avery had felt immensely relieved, but also worried. "Where is she?"

"Gil said she'd gone away on business. She could be busy," Alex reasoned.

Avery just looked at him with raised eyebrows.

Reuben returned to the house with El, and they promised to talk the next day. El said she'd phone Briar with the news. The glasshouse had been sealed off with tape, as had the door to the underground passage, and finally only she and Alex were left.

For a while they sat next to the glasshouse, looking out across the bay to Gull Island. It was late, the sun had set, and a pale moon illuminated their surroundings. Avery wanted to cry again.

"You should stay at my place tonight," Alex said.

"No, I'll be fine," Avery argued, not wanting to put Alex out, even though she really didn't want to be alone.

"All right, I'll put it another way." He reached out to take her hand. He looked tired and sad, and the shadows under his eyes had nothing to do with the darkness. "I want you to stay at my place. I don't want to be alone, and I'll worry about you if you are."

His hand was so warm, and she remembered the comfortable way she had fitted into his hold earlier. She smiled. "In that case, yes please."

So here she was, sleeping in Alex's bed. She replayed everything again and again, and after half an hour of tossing and turning, she fumbled her way to the kitchen in the darkness and poured a glass of water, trying not to disturb Alex.

She heard him stir and he mumbled, "Are you okay?"

"Sorry. I can't sleep."

"Me neither."

"Do you want some water?" She could just see him as her eyes adjusted to the light that trickled in from the street lamps outside.

He sat up, half covered in blankets, his hair loose. "Yes, please."

She finished her water and then carried his glass over, sitting on the edge of the sofa as Alex edged over to make room.

"I'm sorry me and Reuben were gone so long. We could have stopped this," she said. She doubted she would ever forgive herself for yesterday.

Alex finished his drink, put the glass on the coffee table, and then lifted his blanket and threw it over her, pulling her close. His chest was bare and she leaned against him, savouring the warmth and his strong, muscled body. He smelt so good. She immediately felt guilty. *How could she even think this when Gil was dead?*

"Avery, what happened today is not your fault or mine. If you'd been there, you couldn't have surprised Faversham. We might all have been killed."

"Yes, but—"

"No buts."

He leaned in and kissed her, and she thought she might melt right into him. He was intoxicating. She wriggled under him and pulled him closer until they were wrapped around each other, their kisses long and deep. His hands slid up her back under her t-shirt, and she arched against him. And then he started to peel her clothes off, and she decided that staying at Alex's was the best idea ever.

The next time she woke, it was light and they were cocooned in a tangle of blankets. Alex's legs were heavy across her own, his arm wound tightly around her waist. For a few seconds she didn't move, luxuriating in the feeling of him lying next to her.

Her body still tingled from the memory of a few hours ago, and part of her didn't want it to end. She realised that this might have been some grief reaction from him, and if so, she would enjoy it while it lasted. She tried to remember what day it was. *Friday*. Avery groaned. She should phone Sally. She tried to roll gently away from Alex, but his grip tightened and he nuzzled her ear. "Where are you going?"

"I thought I should phone work."

"Bollocks to work."

"I wish. Sally might have heard about Gil by now. I should let her know I'm okay."

"In a minute," he said, kissing the back of her neck and moving on to her shoulder. Immediately, her stomach flipped and she closed her eyes. Sally could wait. After all, she might not even survive the day.

Avery had only been at work for an hour when DI Newton strode purposefully across her shop, the door banging in his wake. She was still upset about Gil, and Sally had burst into tears at the news, which had upset her even more.

Newton's grey eyes bored into hers and he looked grimmer than usual. "Miss Hamilton. We need to talk."

Avery sighed. "Sorry, Sally. I won't be long."

Sally looked between the two of them. "Take as long as you need."

Avery led Newton through the back of the shop and up to her flat. She headed straight to the kitchen and put the kettle on.

"Did you find Alicia?" she asked, her stomach in knots.

"Yes. She'd had her phone turned off."

"Was she upset?"

"What sort of a bloody question is that?" he asked, glaring at her. "Yes. She was upset. She's coming back today. Now, I suggest you tell me what really happened in that cave, because I'm not about to believe the crap you spouted yesterday."

Avery turned her back to him as she prepared the tea and desperately wondered what to say. She had to lie.

"It wasn't crap. Gil had a horrible accident on those old boxes. It's awful, but true."

His voice was scathing. "You're lying. Something terrible is happening in White Haven, and I intend to find out what. I'm on your side, Avery."

"Are you?" she asked, whirling around. "Because it didn't sound like it the other night when we sealed that bloody doorway."

He crossed his arms in front of him and leaned back against the counter, watching her. "All my life I've been hearing about witches, magic, and White Haven, and my place in it. I resisted it then, and I'm resisting it now. Magic should belong in the past."

Avery forgot about the tea. "What are you talking about? What do you know?"

"Not bloody much. What happened, Avery?"

"No! What are you talking about, *your place in it*?"

"Magic runs deep in White Haven. Our history is soaked in it. Something has woken it up. I think that's you."

Avery felt out of her depth. Things were happening that were out of her control, and now it seemed Newton knew more than he was letting on, too. And she still didn't know what to make of Alicia. Her fear made her angry.

"Nothing has *woken up*! I have always had magic, as have the others. You just never cared before, and now you do!"

"Oh, I've always cared," he said, stepping closer. "But nothing bad happened before, and now there have been three deaths in one week!

And all a result of magic and demons. Something has changed, I know it has, and *you* are being obstructive."

Newton's anger was palpable, and she retreated, pressing against the sink. "I'm at a disadvantage here, Newton. You know what I am and what I can do. We sealed that doorway the best we could, and I'll be checking it today. My friend, Gil, is dead. And at this moment, I don't really trust you, despite the fact that you're a detective. You tell me about half-whispered myths, but you don't really share them. So, I'm sticking to what I told you yesterday. We were exploring the tunnels and Gil had a terrible accident, one that I will forever mourn. You don't need to fear me, or Alex, Reuben, Elspeth or Briar, in fact."

"Three deaths, Avery. You should be careful." He gave her one last hard stare and then headed to the door. "I'll be in touch."

Avery watched him leave and felt a wave of despair wash through her. What was happening? They had five grimoires to find, and had only discovered two. Why did Faversham want them? If his magic was so powerful, what could the books offer him and his family? Why had they been hidden at all?

There must be something *else* about the grimoires that was important, something that happened around the time of the Witchfinder. What had Helena and the others done that had earned the enmity of the Favershams? And what had this got to do with Gil's great-uncle Addison?

Avery's thoughts reeled. One thing was certain. Faversham wouldn't stop, and neither would she.

End of Book 1 of the White Haven Witches

Book 2, *Magic Unbound,* is out now, and completes this story. All other books in this series are complete stories.
You can buy it here: https://books2read.com/magic-unbound Read on for an excerpt.

If you enjoyed this book and would like to read more of my stories, please subscribe to my newsletter at tjgreenauthor.com. You will get two free short stories, *Excalibur Rises* and *Jack's Encounter*, and will also receive free character sheets of all the main White Haven witches.

Excerpt of Magic Unbound

A very waited impatiently outside the Witch Museum. It was 2:30 in the morning, and the small town of White Haven was quiet, other than the sound of unearthly grunts and snarls that came from inside the building. The devil's trap had caught something, and the warning she had set up had triggered, waking her from a fitful night's sleep. Any minute now, the other witches would arrive.

It was Sunday night, three nights after Gil's death, and Avery felt gritty-eyed and sleep deprived. If she was honest, she was happy to be woken by the need to do something useful. His death had left her tossing and turning, pondering what-ifs and maybes. She hadn't seen the others since then.

Avery glanced nervously around the car park. If that was a demon in the museum, and it certainly sounded like one, someone had summoned it. If it was Faversham, and she was convinced it must be, was he close by, or doing this from a distance?

As she looked towards the town, she saw shadows edge across the car park. It was the other witches, and she sighed with relief.

Alex blinked back tiredness. "How long?"

"Thirty minutes at most," she said, adjusting her backpack with her grimoire in it.

Briar nodded in acknowledgement. "I can't believe the trap worked. I've got goose bumps." She looked around. "No Reuben?"

Avery shook her head. "No. I didn't think we should disturb him. Have you seen him, El?"

"No. He doesn't want to see anyone right now." El seemed like she was trying to sound cool about it, but Avery detected a tightness in her voice that wasn't normally there.

"Fair enough," Alex nodded. "Let's get on with it. I've brought my new grimoire—there's a spell that I think will work."

"Excellent," Avery said, "because my idea feels shaky. And guys, someone must have summoned that demon. They may still be here." She turned to the back door and with a whispered spell, the door unlocked and they slipped into the museum.

The smell of blood and mustiness was heavy in the air, but stronger than that was the scent of sulphur. The noise in here was louder, too, and her skin pricked at the feral, inhuman sounds that came from inside the main room. A flickering orange light illuminated the doorway.

"What's causing that?" El whispered.

"We'll soon find out," Alex said, leading the way.

A shudder ran down Avery's spine as she saw the dark, multi-limbed, writhing shape, bursting against the constraints of the devil's trap. As the demon saw them enter the room, it howled, revealing a large mouth filled with sharp teeth, and its blood red eyes fixed them with a piercing stare. On the wall behind it was the occult doorway that it had travelled through. The sigils were alight with flames, and acrid smoke poured off them; Avery could see indistinct shapes lurking in the other dimension.

"May the Great Goddess protect us," Briar whispered. She stood, making her personal preparations that Avery was slowly becoming familiar with. She removed her shoes and stood barefoot, grounding herself ready to draw the Earth's strength.

Alex pulled his grimoire free and set it up on a small display case, working quickly and surely, while El pulled a short sword out of her pack and stood poised, ready to strike.

Avery watched them with interest. "What's with the sword, El?"

"After you used the ceremonial sword successfully the other night to help you channel air, I thought I would bind this one with fire—it's smaller and easier to carry, and there's a little something extra in there, too." She grimaced. "Fun times."

"Well, that's one way of putting it."

"Alex, if your banishing spells don't work, what's the back-up plan?" El asked.

"A shit-storm of elemental magic?" Alex glanced up from the pages. "I've got this. Trust me. Just give me one more minute."

Avery took deep, calming breaths and tried to focus. Magic worked best with a clear head and a definite plan. While she waited for Alex, Avery watched the demon. The last time they had encountered them, it had been impossible to study them properly, but now that this one was trapped, she could take her time. Like the other demons, it was made of fire and smoke, its form threatening but seemingly insubstantial. However, this one was bigger, with more limbs. Power radiated from it. It writhed so quickly, it was difficult to make out its complete form, or if it even had one. It seemed to constantly shift, one limb morphing into another, and its eyes moved around within what she assumed was its head. It snapped its huge, gaping mouth, revealing long, sharp teeth, and its growls of frustration were like hearing nails scraped down a blackboard. Fire whips struck against the trap's invisible walls, desperately trying to reach them.

Behind it, the occult doorway was fascinating, fire blazing across its runes and sigils. She wondered if the trapped demon meant the doorway couldn't close.

Alex shouted, "I'm ready! Repeat after me."

They linked hands and Alex started his spell. It was written in archaic English, and at first he stumbled over the words, but then he became more confident and they repeated the words together, each cycle growing in power and conviction.

The demon writhed even more furiously, its shape changing too quickly to register. Avery almost stepped back, its ferocity was so scary, but she held her ground and raised her voice, finding strength in its desperate attempts to escape.

Then, with an almighty crack, the invisible walls of the devil's trap shattered and a rope of flames streaked across the room, whipped around Briar's ankle, and pulled her towards the doorway. It seemed the trap still had some power as the demon stayed within its circle, but more and more flame ropes lashed towards them.

Briar slithered across the floor screaming and trying to break free, hurling energy bolts at the demon, but it was too strong.

El loosed Avery's hand and ran across the room, wielding her sword that now flashed with a white flame.

Avery wavered for a moment, but Alex tightened his grip on her hand, repeating the spell, and she drew on her power once again, binding her strength with his as they repeated the words faster and faster.

El sliced and hacked at the flame ropes, moving with athletic fury. The ropes shrivelled as she cut them, but she still couldn't get to Briar who was being pulled closer and closer to the demon. She renewed her attack, and Avery tried not to lose concentration. Finally El sliced through the flame rope holding Briar, just as she reached the edge of the trap.

With an insidious whisper, the doorway changed and they all almost faltered. Avery had thought it was open before, but as their spell started to work, the runes faded away, revealing the dimension in all its horror. It was like staring into a gigantic whirlpool of fire that stretched back aeons—it was time that Avery sensed, not space, and it was terrifying.

El grabbed Briar and hauled her across the room, both of them stumbling in their haste.

But the doorway was open for mere seconds. It sucked the demon back within its realms and the doorway shut with a resounding roar, plunging them into darkness.

For a second no one moved, and then Avery spelled a ball of witch light into her hands and threw it up towards the ceiling where it floated, illuminating the space below.

"Everyone okay?" Avery asked. Her heart pounded in her chest, and she felt a little dizzy.

Alex stood immobile, and then he grinned. "Hell yeah! I just banished a demon and closed a dimension—don't thank me all at once!"

"I meant El and Briar," she said with a raised eyebrow. "But well done. It was very impressive."

"Impressive? It was bloody awesome!"

Avery winked at him. "Only kidding. It's interesting that your grimoire has such spells."

Briar interrupted them. "Don't worry about us—I only almost got sucked into some infernal dimension. El, thank you. You were brilliant." Briar looked pale, and she held her hands over her ankle and calf for a few seconds, murmuring a spell. "That really hurts. It would have been a lot worse without my jeans on."

El smiled and looked at her sword. "This worked better than I thought."

"So what was your special something in the sword?" Avery asked.

"Ice fire."

"Is that even a thing?"

"It is now. Demons don't like it."

"Wow. This night is so weird."

Alex stepped closer to the closed occult doorway, pulling a large potion bottle out of his pocket. "One final thing." He opened the bottle and threw the contents over the doorway with a final incantation, and the runes and marks started to fade until they completely disappeared. "Done. Nothing's coming out of that again."

El looked puzzled. "But who summoned the demon? Where are they?"

Alex shrugged. "Maybe it was done from a distance. Wherever they are, they were trying to disrupt White Haven."

"Maybe it's a distraction," Avery suggested.

"From what?" El asked. "We've protected everything we can."

Briar stood and joined them. "Maybe whoever did this thought the demon would kill one of us. We're too good. I finally feel like we have a win."

"Come on," Alex said. "Let's clean up this place and get out of here."

"Wait," Avery said, moving towards the shattered display next to where the doorway had been. It hadn't been changed since the night they were last here. Underneath the broken glass was a simple ink line drawing depicting Helena, tied to the stake. She was wrapped in a cloak, and her dark hair was flying around her face as if a strong wind was blowing. A man leant forward with a burning branch to light the pyre beneath. Around the pyre, a group of people watched.

Avery shuddered. *Poor Helena*. She thought back to their interview with Samuel Kingston. *What if she had been betrayed?* Avery had to find out.

Next to the picture was a display of objects used on an altar. There was an Athame, ancient and worn, its blade dull, the hilt patterned with an old Celtic design. Next to it was an engraved chalice, a ritual bowl made of silver, and two pillar candles that had once been lit. There were two dishes made out of carved wood, the traces of what Avery presumed was salt in one, the other traditionally used for water. The objects were laid out symmetrically on a white cotton cloth, all sealed within a glass-framed display case. Bundles of plants were lined up at the back of the altar, and Avery recognised bay leaves, rowan berries, acorns, oak leaves, and a spiral of hazel branches. She smiled, realising that it really was an altar, placed here many years ago, Helena watching over it.

An old leather book lay to the side, filled with pages of writing. It looked like a ledger, and underneath it was a sign that read: "Final sales records from Helena Marchmont's business." Avery flicked through the pages with avid curiosity. *Had this been written by Helena's own hand?* As the witch light glowed from above, a silvery shape began to appear on the open pages in the centre of the book. Avery gasped. It was a message.

No, it was a map.

She reached forward, brushing away shards of glass and reached in for the book.

"What's up, Avery?" Alex asked, coming to stand next to her.

"Look!" She lifted the book and turned it under the light. "It's a map."

He leaned in closer. "A map! Of what?"

She shook her head. "I don't know."

El and Briar joined them, Briar smiling. "This has been here all these years, waiting for you to find it."

"Could it show us where her grimoire is?" Alex asked.

"What else could it be?"

For the first time in days, Avery felt a spark of excitement run through her. After Gil's death, nothing had seemed worth it. Even banishing the demon and closing the doorway, although important, had weighed upon her shoulders. She had questioned what they were doing, and wondered if it was worth the risk. But it had to be. The path to her grimoire was right in front of her.

Buy it here: https://books2read.com/magic-unbound

Author's Note

T hank you for reading *Buried Magic,* the first book in the White Haven Witches Series.

I love stories about witches and magic, and I love Cornwall, so I decided to put the two together! White Haven is a fictional town, but reflects the beauty of the beautiful Cornwall fishing villages and the surrounding area. Harecombe, the base of Faversham Central, is also fictional.

The Royal Cornwall Museum and the Courtney Library are real, but the archive is my fictional addition.

Of course, there really was a Witchfinder General who was responsible for many deaths, but he never made it to Cornwall - that's another bit of fiction.

I have lots of people to thank for their help with this book.

Thanks to Fiona Jayde Media for my awesome cover, and thanks to Kyla Stein at Missed Period Editing for ironing out the kinks!

I also must thank Helen Ryan and Terri Cormack for their fantastic feedback on my first draft which prompted a very important rewrite - you're both awesome!

Thanks also to my launch team, who give valuable feedback on typos and are happy to review on release. It's lovely to hear from them - you know who you are - and their feedback is always so encouraging.

I'm lucky to have them on my team! I love hearing from all my readers, so I welcome you to get in touch.

Thanks of course to my partner, Jason, who does most of the cooking while I'm feverishly writing in the study. Without his unfailing support and encouragement, my life would be so much harder - and I'd starve.

I've dedicated this book to my mother, because not only is she one of my biggest fans, but also because I think there's a little bit of witch in all of us, and as the matriarchal head of the family, she's offered plenty of good advice over the years - and plenty of uncanny insight! Thanks mom!

If you'd like to read a bit more background to the stories, please head to my website, tjgreenauthor.com, where I'll be blogging about the books I've read and the research I've done on the series - in fact there's lots of stuff on there about my other series, Tom's Arthurian Legacy, too.

If you'd like to read more of my writing, please join my mailing list. You can get a free short story called *Jack's Encounter*, describing how Jack met Fahey – a longer version of the prologue in *Tom's Inheritance* – by subscribing to my newsletter. You'll also get a FREE copy of *Excalibur Rises*, a short story prequel.

You will also receive free character sheets on all of my main characters in White Haven Witches - exclusive to my email list!

By staying on my mailing list you'll receive free excerpts of my new books, as well as short stories and news of giveaways. I'll also be sharing information about other books in this genre you might enjoy.

Give me my FREE short stories!

I look forward to you joining my readers' group.

About the Author

I grew up in England and now live in the Hutt Valley, near Wellington, New Zealand, with my partner Jason, and my cats Sacha and Leia. When I'm not writing, you'll find me with my head in a book, gardening, or doing yoga. And maybe getting some retail therapy!

In a previous life I've been a singer in a band, and have done some acting with a theatre company – both of which were lots of fun. On occasions I make short films with a few friends, which begs the question, where are the book trailers? Thinking on it ...

I'm currently working on more books in the White Haven Witches series, musing on a prequel, and planning for a fourth book in Tom's Arthurian Legacy series.

Please follow me on social media to keep up to date with my news, or join my mailing list - I promise I don't spam! Join my mailing list here.

For more information, please visit my website, as well as Facebook, Twitter, Pinterest, Goodreads, BookBub, and Instagram.

Also By

Rise of the King Series

A Young Adult series about a teen called Tom who's summoned to wake King Arthur. It's a fun adventure about King Arthur in the Otherworld!

Call of the King #1

King Arthur is destined to return, and Tom is destined to wake him.

When sixteen year old Tom's grandfather mysteriously disappears, Tom stops at nothing to find him, even when that means crossing to a mysterious and unknown world.

When he gets there, Tom discovers that everything he thought he knew about himself and his life was wrong. Vivian, the Lady of the Lake, has been watching over him and manipulating his life since his birth. And now she needs his help.

The Silver Tower #2

Merlin disappeared over a thousand years ago. Now they risk everything to find him. Vivian needs King Arthur's help. Nimue, a powerful witch and priestess who lives on Avalon, has disappeared.

King Arthur, Tom, and his friends set off across the Other to find her, following Nimue's trail to Nimue seems to have a quest of her own, one she's deliberately hiding. Arthur is convinced it's about Merlin, and he's determined to find him.

The Cursed Sword #3

An ancient sword. A dark secret. A new enemy.

Tom loves his new life in the Otherworld. He lives with Arthur in New Camelot, and Arthur is hosting a tournament. Eager to test his sword-fighting skills, Tom's competing.

But while the games are being played, his friends are attacked and everything he loves is threatened. Tom has to find the intruder before anyone else gets hurt.

Tom's sword seems to be the focus of these attacks. Their investigations uncover its dark history and a terrible betrayal that a family has kept secret for generations.

White Haven Hunters

A spin-off set in the White Haven world which starts after Crossroads Magic, book 6 in the White Haven Witches series. Details on my website- www.tjgreenauthor.com